*Brady wanted a woman to scream for him...*

And after downing four beers, followed by a champagne chaser at the Pink Cadillac a few hours earlier, the solution to Brady's problem suddenly became clear. He'd find a woman and satisfy her fifty ways 'til Sunday.

But not just any woman would do. It had to be the woman who'd always managed to get him hot and bothered when he was younger, the woman who'd haunted his dreams since he left town. Eden Hallsey, Cadillac's resident bad girl. If he could satisfy Eden, then he would know, deep down in his soul, that his ex-wife had been lying.

Just the thought of Eden brought to mind a vision of her as she'd been tonight, staring up at him in the hallway of the bar, her lips plump and parted, desire gleaming in her eyes. Brady's groin tightened and he shifted in the bed to make himself more comfortable.

Yes, he was going to sleep with Eden Hallsey. And prove to the world, once and for all, that he was every bit a man.

D0802837

Dear Reader,

Harlequin Blaze is a supersexy new series. If you like love stories with a strong sexual edge, then this is the line for you! The books are fun and flirtatious, the heroes are hot and outrageous. Blaze is a series for the woman who wants *more* in her reading pleasure....

This month, *USA Today* bestselling author JoAnn Ross brings you #5 *Thirty Nights,* a provocative story about a man who wants a woman for only thirty nights of sheer pleasure. Then popular Kimberly Raye poses the question of what women really expect in a man, in the sizzling #6 *The Pleasure Principle.* Talented Candace Schuler delivers #7 *Uninhibited,* a hot story with two fiery protagonists who have few inhibitions—about each other! Carly Phillips rounds out the month with another SEXY CITY NIGHTS story set in New York—where the heat definitely escalates after dark...

Look for four Blaze books every month at your favorite bookstore. And check us out online at eHarlequin.com and tryblaze.com.

Enjoy!

Birgit Davis-Todd
Senior Editor & Editorial Coordinator
Harlequin Blaze

# THE PLEASURE PRINCIPLE

*Kimberly Raye*

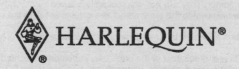

TORONTO • NEW YORK • LONDON
AMSTERDAM • PARIS • SYDNEY • HAMBURG
STOCKHOLM • ATHENS • TOKYO • MILAN • MADRID
PRAGUE • WARSAW • BUDAPEST • AUCKLAND

For Brenna Evelyn Groff,
My little miracle from above. Mommy loves you!
And, as always, for Curt, Brenna's wonderful father
and the man of my dreams.
I feel truly blessed.

ISBN 0-373-79010-4

THE PLEASURE PRINCIPLE

Copyright © 2001 by Kimberly Raye Rangel.

All rights reserved. Except for use in any review, the reproduction or
utilization of this work in whole or in part in any form by any electronic,
mechanical or other means, now known or hereafter invented, including
xerography, photocopying and recording, or in any information storage
or retrieval system, is forbidden without the written permission of the
publisher, Harlequin Enterprises Limited, 225 Duncan Mill Road,
Don Mills, Ontario, Canada M3B 3K9.

All characters in this book have no existence outside the imagination of
the author and have no relation whatsoever to anyone bearing the same
name or names. They are not even distantly inspired by any individual
known or unknown to the author, and all incidents are pure invention.

This edition published by arrangement with Harlequin Books S.A.

® and TM are trademarks of the publisher. Trademarks indicated with
® are registered in the United States Patent and Trademark Office, the
Canadian Trade Marks Office and in other countries.

Visit us at www.eHarlequin.com

Printed in U.S.A.

## ABOUT THE AUTHOR...

Kimberly Raye has always been an incurable romantic, so she considers romance writing the perfect job for her. Especially when all her books feature her favorite type of hero—a rough-and-tough cowboy with tight jeans and a killer smile! Kim lives in the Lone Star State with her very own cowboy, her young son, Joshua, and her brand-new baby girl, Brenna.

For those of you who enjoy *The Pleasure Principle*, you won't want to miss the prequel! Get to know Eden Hallsey and the townspeople of Cadillac, Texas, in *Show and Tell*, Kim's contribution to *Midnight Fantasies*, the 2001 Blaze Collection, which hit the stands in July.

## Books by Kimberly Raye

**HARLEQUIN TEMPTATION**
728—BREATHLESS
791—SHAMELESS
807—RESTLESS

# 1

AS OWNER AND OPERATOR of the only bar in Cadillac, Texas, Eden Hallsey came into contact with more than her fair share of men. Males of all shapes and sizes—rich and poor, young and old, annoying and nice, homely and handsome. But never had she seen one as handsome, as sexy, as *hot* as the man standing on the side of the road, next to a steaming black Porsche.

*Handsome,* as in short, dark hair that framed a *GQ* face, complete with a straight nose and strong jaw and sensual lips.

*Sexy,* as in the sensual way his white dress shirt outlined his muscular shoulders and broad chest, while soft, black trousers accented a trim waist and molded to his hips.

*Hot* as in the beads of perspiration that clung to his forehead, slid down his cheeks, the tanned column of his throat. He wiped his brow as he lifted a hand to flag her down.

Before she even realized what she was doing,

her foot shifted to the brake and she started to slow. A few seconds later, she pulled up in front of the sleek sports car and rolled down her window.

"Need some help?" she asked as he walked up. She reached beneath the seat for the Triple A kit her waitress and friend Kasey had given her last Christmas. A click and she started rummaging in the tackle-size box. "Let's see. I've got jumper cables. A jack. Spare can of oil." A girl had to be prepared, as Kasey always said. Of course, in this situation her friend would have been referring to the tube of Passionate Pink lipstick she'd taped inside the top of the tackle box.

Eden barely ignored the urge to grab the tube and rub some of the color on her lips. Eden Hallsey primped for no man, even one as handsome as this one.

"Pick your poison," she told him after she'd licked her lips and ticked off the remaining contents of the box.

"A gun would be nice."

Her head snapped up and her gaze collided with his. She realized he looked vaguely familiar as her breath caught and her mouth actually went dry at the sight of the most intense, vivid blue eyes she'd ever seen.

A crazy reaction, because Eden's mouth never went dry over a man. Sure, she appreciated the opposite sex. She even enjoyed them on occasion—though the last being so long ago she could hardly remember. She liked men, all right, as everyone well knew. But she never, *ever* let any one man get to her.

*Until this man.*

She ignored the crazy thought and concentrated on finding her voice. "Pardon?"

His grin was slow and easy and as breath-stealing as the record-breaking hundred degree heat baking the surrounding stretch of pasture. "To put her out of her misery." He motioned behind him. "The engine block is cracked and nothing short of a miracle is likely to revive her."

She couldn't help but return his smile. "Sorry, but I'm fresh out of miracles today."

His grin faltered and something passed in his gaze. "Me, too. Thankfully."

His last comment, coupled with the flash of relief in his blue eyes, made her think that Mr. Handsome, Sexy and Hot wasn't all that disappointed to see his fifty-thousand-dollar car steaming in the midday heat.

The thought passed as he turned his attention back to her. A hungry light fired his gaze and her breath caught. It was a look she was all too familiar with since she'd given her virginity to Jake Marlboro back in high school. He'd violated her trust and turned what should have been something beautiful into a tawdry good time to brag about to his friends. Thus, her reputation had been born and she'd endured it ever since. The bold pick-up lines, the raunchy comments, the hungry looks.

But this was different. Her response was different. She didn't just want to slap his face. She wanted to throw her arms around him and see if his lips felt as soft and mesmerizing as they looked.

"If you don't mind, I could really use a ride."

The last word lingered in her head and stirred a vivid image of him stretched out on her flower print sheets, his body dark and masculine and hard beneath her.

"But if it makes you uncomfortable, I could just walk."

But that was the kicker. The notion of giving him a ride, in or out of bed, didn't make her uncomfortable in the least.

Just hot.

"I'd be happy to help." The words were out before she could consider that the man was a stranger, no matter how familiar he looked. He could be a serial killer for all she knew. A Porsche-driving, Gucci-wearing madman.

Then again, she'd been on blind dates that looked far more scary and intimidating. This guy was neither, and her gut told her he wasn't dangerous either—except to her hormones. But she could maintain control of herself for the five minutes it would take to drive him to Merle's Service Station.

Eden Hallsey *always* kept her control. She was notorious for it. She was notorious for a *lot* of things.

"I really wouldn't want to put you out," he went on, mistaking her silence for hesitation.

"You're not. You're the one who'll be inconvenienced. I'm afraid the closest gas station is about two miles straight into town."

"It's no inconvenience. That's where I was headed."

His words surprised her. She'd figured he'd pulled off the interstate near the town's only exit out of pure necessity, not by choice. They didn't see many of his type in a desperately small town like Cadillac. Not that the place didn't have it's share of wealth. Cadillac was home to two of the largest ranches in Texas, not to mention Weston Boots, the oldest and largest western boot manufacturer in the country. But the wealthy were still just locals. Country folk. Men like old Zachariah Weston and rancher Silver Dollar Sam—so named because of the silver dollars he handed out to the kiddies when he played Santa Claus at the yearly winter festival. While they might drive fancy utility vehicles and wear solid gold belt buckles, they still spent their Saturday nights having ice cream at the Dairy Freeze right alongside everybody else.

Her gaze shifted to the man standing outside her truck window, with his expensive Italian suit and his elite sports car. Again, a strange sense of familiarity hit her, as if she'd seen him in this exact pose before.

She shook away the crazy thought and reached over to unlock the opposite door. If she had come into contact with him before, she couldn't imagine ever forgetting. He was too handsome, too sexy, too stirring.

Then again, maybe she was remembering. A memory from long ago. A man who'd been just a boy...

She searched her mind as he climbed in beside her. But then the door closed and his scent surrounded her, and her thoughts scattered. Her heart pounded and her stomach jumped and it was all she could do to concentrate on pulling away from the shoulder of the road, out onto the main strip leading into town.

"So," she licked her lips and tried to calm her thundering heart, "are you visiting friends in town? Family?"

"Both." He didn't spare her a glance as he drank in the passing scenery, as if he were seeing pastureland and farmhouses for the very first time. "At least I hope so."

"Have you ever been to Cadillac before?" she asked, eager to satisfy the curiosity bubbling inside her.

"Yes." He didn't offer any more information, telling Eden as plain as day, that he wasn't as interested in getting to know her as she was in getting to know him, despite the openly hungry look he'd directed at her earlier.

It seemed that not only had her response to this man strayed from her usual indifference, *he* was acting different from most men. Any other man would have taken the opportunity to flirt and tease and even openly proposition her should they have found themselves alone with her in the close confines of her truck.

Not that Eden was some irresistible beauty queen. Far from it. It wasn't her average looks that made her attractive to men. It was the rumors.

She'd learned over the years that a woman with a reputation was like a plate of free cookies. Even if a person wasn't hungry, they reached for a sweet just because it was there and it was free and everybody else was taking some.

It was a fact of life. Men flirted with her. All men. Her gaze snagged on the man seated next to her. The guy didn't so much as spare her a glance. Okay, so make that most men.

Then again, if he wasn't from around these parts he didn't know her or her reputation. As far as he was concerned, she was just another woman.

Eden bit her bottom lip to keep from asking him more questions. He didn't want to talk and she wasn't going to make a pest of herself no matter how much she suddenly wanted to know everything about him, from his name to his likes and dislikes. Instead, she fixed her attention on trying to place him in her memory. He'd admitted that he'd been to Cadillac before. Maybe she had seen him. Eden was still searching her memory when they pulled into Merle's Gas-n-Go.

"Thanks," he said as he started to climb out, that same preoccupied look in his gaze that made Eden wonder yet again if she'd only imagined that initial hungry look he'd given her.

"Wait," she said as he moved to close the door.

"Don't forget your duffel bag...." The words faded as she leaned over to grab his bag and her gaze snagged on the worn boots he was wearing—*worn* when the rest of him was polished to the max. The heel had the familiar trademark *W* branded into its side.

An image rushed at her of a blue-jean-clad senior with long legs and an easy smile. He'd worn a similar pair of boots as he'd stood on the side of the road next to his granddaddy's pickup, one of the rear tires as flat as Jamie McGee's hair after a good ironing.

Eden's head snapped up and her eyes collided with his. "Brady Weston. You're *Brady Weston.*" *The* Brady Weston. The boy who'd been every girl's dream, Eden's included.

His grin was as slow and as warm as she remembered on that hot July day when she'd given him her tire jack and a long swallow of her ice-cold Coke.

"The last time I looked."

"It *is* you." Her heart pumped ninety-to-nothing at the realization. "Y-you probably don't recognize me. I'm—"

"Eden Hallsey," he finished for her. "I'd know your smile anywhere. Thanks for saving me. Again." Then, with a wink, he closed the door and

Eden was left with the startling knowledge that after a bitter fight with his grandaddy and an eleven-year absence, Brady Weston—the captain of the hockey team, the heir to the Weston boot fortune and the star of Eden's wildest adolescent fantasies—had finally come home.

HE WAS HOME.

Reality hit Brady as he stood before Merle's gas station and stared at the fading red sign that hung in front. The same painted oval that had always teetered back and forth from two small chains. The edges were a little more worn than he remembered, the paint chipped in several spots, but otherwise it was exactly the same. The same name with the same familiar twenty-four hour service guarantee printed just below. A red-and-white T-ball banner flapped in the wind depicting one of the local teams in the peewee league. The same team—the Kansas City Royals—that Merle's station sponsored each and every year.

Thankfully.

Brady had seen too many new barns, new fences, even a few new houses dotting the horizon on the drive into town and the scenery had made him worry that maybe things had changed too much for him to simply waltz back home after all these years and pick up where he'd left off.

And he wanted to. Christ, he wanted it more than his next breath of air.

He glanced behind him at the familiar span of buildings lining main street, from Turtle Jim's Diner, where he'd eaten chili cheese fries after school every Friday afternoon, to Sullivan's Pharmacy, where he'd purchased his very first condom. The breath he'd been holding eased from his lungs and he drank in another lungful of Texas heat.

*Home.*

He'd dreamt about this moment so many times over the past eleven years, when the stress of a fast-paced advertising career and a less than perfect home life had overwhelmed him and he'd longed for the peace he'd known while growing up. The freedom. The control.

He'd been the one in control back then. But for the past eleven years, life and circumstance and his ex-wife had called the shots, dictating the how, when and where.

Only because he'd allowed it, he reminded himself. It wasn't as if he'd been forced away from Cadillac. He'd fallen in love, or so he'd thought at the time, and walked away by choice—to do the right thing. In the end, however, everything he'd done that fateful day and every moment since had been wrong. So wrong.

Not now. Not ever again.

The past was just that—the past. Over. Finished. Bye, bye. It was the future that mattered now, and Brady wasn't making any more mistakes. Rather, he was finally going to set things right.

He ran a hand through his sweat-dampened hair and spared a glance around him. A handful of kids were gathered around a nearby candy machine at the far corner of the building. Brady turned, letting his gaze sweep the other side. The gleam of an old-fashioned Coke machine caught his eye and he smiled. Yep, Cadillac was still good old Cadillac.

Sliding a coin into the slot, he pushed the same button he'd pushed every day after school since the moment he'd been tall enough to swipe quarters from the top of his older sister's dresser once she'd left for school in the morning.

The machine grumbled, then stalled the way it always had for several long moments before finally spitting out a bottle of Orange Crush. He popped the tab and lifted the opening to his lips. Anticipation rolled through him, thirst coiled in his stomach—familiar feelings that he'd felt every time he'd stood in this very same spot with his favorite drink.

Yet, at the same time, he felt different. Hotter. More anxious. Downright *needy*.

Thanks to Eden Hallsey.

He took a long swig of soda, but it did little to ease his body temperature which had soared the moment she'd pulled up in her beat-up Chevy to rescue him from his own stupidity.

At first, he'd been convinced she was a mirage. He'd been stranded on the highway just miles from his hometown. It only made sense that he would conjure the sexiest girl from his past.

But then she'd touched him, just a soft gesture on his hand, and every nerve in his body had jumped to awareness. In a matter of seconds, he'd been as hard as an iron spike.

He'd reacted the same way on their one and only date. That had been before Sally, or rather, before his head had lost the battle with his hormones, he'd fancied himself in love and had forgotten to wear a condom on one of their dates. She'd gotten pregnant and they'd gotten married, and his dating days had been over. She'd lost the baby shortly after, but it was too late. He'd taken sacred vows, and he *had* loved her, or so he'd thought at the time, and she'd claimed to love him. He'd believed her, up until six months ago when she'd run off with one of his business associates.

So much for love.

But before…

There'd been Eden Hallsey. From tenth grade on, she'd been the prettiest and sexiest girl around and the fantasy of every boy at Cadillac, Brady included. He'd heard every rumor about her, and while he didn't believe them all—he'd known her before tenth grade—when she'd been shy and naïve and a nice girl—he knew there was at least a kernel of truth. She *was* sexy.

And he'd wanted her.

The date had been nothing more than tradition. He'd been the star prize in the yearly football lottery, where girls bought tickets for a chance to win a date with their favorite jock. He'd been surprised to see her raise her hand when the number had been called. After all, Eden hadn't needed to buy a ticket to get a date. She could have any guy. But she'd bought a ticket for him. For a few seconds, he'd been excited until a friend had alerted him to the fact that she was making her way through the football team and he was the last on her list. Just another conquest.

Oddly enough, he hadn't wanted to be another in a long line. He'd wanted to be different. To stand out, and so he'd done what no other guy had

ever been able to do—he'd kept his distance.
Barely.

That had been a long time ago. His hormones
had never been more out of control than at this
time, or so he'd thought until he'd climbed into the
cab beside her today. He might as well have been
sixteen again, with raging needs and a permanent
hard-on. The reaction was the same. Fierce. Immediate.

Thankfully, that reaction had jolted some common sense into him. He'd let his passion get him
into trouble before. He'd lost everything because
of one night and it wasn't happening again just
because Eden was every bit as luscious as he remembered. He wouldn't screw things up again before he'd even had the chance to set them right.

A chance. That's why Brady was back in Cadillac. He wanted a chance to reclaim his old life.
A chance to make amends for mistaking lust for
love and beg his grandfather's forgiveness for for-
saking his family for a girl who'd never really
loved him.

Not that love had been the sole deciding factor
that had figured into his decision to forfeit an all
expense paid education at Texas A & M for two
jobs and community college in Dallas. Duty had
been a part of his decision as well. And responsi-

bility. And commitment. They were the reasons Brady had left.

The reasons he'd finally come back.

"Say there, son. Can I help..." The words trailed off as astonishment lit the old man's face as he walked around the corner of the building. He wore faded jean overalls and a worn Kansas City Royals T-shirt beneath it. Salt-and-pepper hair framed a wrinkled face, and a matching mustache twitched on his upper lip. "Why, I declare. Brady Zachariah Weston! Is that you, you ole sonofa-gun?"

"It's me, all right." He took the older man's hand for a hearty shake. "It's good to see you, Unc."

Merle Weston was Brady's great uncle, his grandfather's little brother, and the classic black sheep of the Weston clan. For as long as Brady could remember, Merle had been the outsider. He'd declined any part of the Weston boot business and opened up his own gas station some thirty-odd years ago, despite his older brother's fierce objections. After all, Weston Boots was a family affair and Zachariah Weston didn't take too kindly to his kin going against family tradition.

Brady knew that firsthand.

Merle had never seemed to care, however. If

anything, he'd gone out of his way just to stay at odds with his older brother. He'd traded the family business and fortune for his own service station that barely made ends meet.

He'd married the wrong woman, at least according to his older brother whose definition of right involved money—lots of money. And he'd moved clear across town, away from the family ranch that still housed three generations of Westons.

The older man scratched the side of his head with a faded, rolled-up issue of *Popular Mechanics*. "Why, I was wonderin' when you'd finally make it back—hey, there!" His attention shifted to the kids poking around the candy machine. "You young'uns either put some change in or skeedadle, otherwise I'll take a hickory switch to every single one of you!" He turned back to Brady and his face split into a grin. "You're lookin' awful good, son. A little slick," he said, his gaze sweeping Brady from head to toe as he let out a low whistle. "Awful fancy threads you got there."

"One of the hazards of working in Dallas. I see you're still too cheap to spring for a current edition of *Popular Mechanics*." He indicated the rolled-up magazine.

"The back issues I get from the beauty parlor every six months when Eula cleans off her coffee table are plenty good enough for me.'' He winked. ''What can I say? The price is right.''

''There is no price.''

''That's why it's so right. I ain't made of money like some folks around here.'' He winked. ''Speaking of which, I heard you're headin' up one of them highfalutin ad agencies out there.''

''*Was*. I'm through doing the corporate thing. I want to slow down. Speaking of which, my car quit on me out on the highway. You think you could dig up a wrecker and give me a tow?''

''Sure thing. What kind of car?''

''Black.''

''I'm talking make and model.''

Brady drew in a deep breath. ''A Porsche 366.''

Merle let loose another whistle. ''Slick car to go with the duds.''

''Not for long. These clothes are a mite too hot for me. I'm thinking of changing before I head over to Granddaddy's place.''

''You sure as hell better. He's still a little attached to his Wranglers, and anybody who ain't wearin' them amounts to an outsider.''

''I've got a pair in my suitcase.'' Several pairs to be more exact. While Brady had left straight from his office and hadn't taken the time to change, he had come as prepared as possible to face his grandfather after all these years.

"Since my car's out of commission, you have any loaners you can spare?"

"All's I got is ole Bessie out back."

"You mean she actually still runs?" Brady remembered the old Chevy pickup being on its last legs back when he was in high school.

"On occasion. She's pretty reliable, so long as you stroke the console 'afore you start her."

"Will do."

"I don't think your grandfather will take too kindly to you driving up in Bessie."

True enough, but Zachariah would like it even less seeing his only grandson drive up in a fancy car the likes of which no salt-of-the-earth cowboy would be caught dead in.

"A truck's a truck. So," Brady went on, eager to change the subject, "you're looking really good. Still sponsoring the same T-ball team and wearing the same shirt."

"It ain't the same. They give me a new one every year. One of the perks. As a matter of fact, I made 'em give me two shirts this past year 'cause I hit my twenty-year mark."

Brady grinned. "Still spittin' vinegar, I see."

Merle winked before casting a glance at the kids

and giving them a look that sent them running. "And pissin' fire," he added, turning back to Brady. "Thanks to Maria's cookin'."

"She still make the best tamales this side of the Rio Grande?"

"And the best dadburned enchiladas. I keep tellin' her she ought to put all that good cookin' to use and open up a restaurant. Then I could retire and let Marlboro have this old place."

"Jake Marlboro?"

He nodded. "He's been itchin' to buy me out all year. Already talked Cecil over at McIntyre Hardware into selling his place."

"Why would he want the old hardware store?"

"He's fixing on putting in a Mega Mart. It's got everything from hardware to groceries. Opened one up over in Inspiration and it's a big hit. Folks like the convenience, I guess. Me, I'm just a little attached to this place. Not to mention, I ain't sold Maria on the restaurant idea. She says she's too busy with all the young'uns."

"How many are you up to?"

"Out of seven grandkids, we've got nineteen great-grandbabies, and number twenty's due any day now." A smile creased his old face. "Your gramps is pickle green with envy."

"And you're loving every minute of it."

Merle's grin widened. "I never had too many chances to one-up your old grandpa when we were growing up, and I ain't ashamed to admit that it's a mite satisfying to know there's something the old coot wants that he cain't have." At Brady's smile, Merle shrugged. "What can I say? Things ain't changed much in the past eleven years."

Brady sent up a silent prayer. "That's what I'm counting on."

# 2

"BRADY'S HOME!" The shout preceded the frantic embrace of Brady's youngest sister. Before he could so much as get in a hello, she opened the front door, threw herself into his arms and held on for dear life.

For the next few moments, Brady forgot his doubts and simply relished the feeling. It had been a long time since he'd been hugged so fiercely...since he'd wanted to hug so fiercely.

"You're here," his sister murmured into his shoulder. "You're really here." Another quick squeeze and she pulled back enough to give him a scolding look. "It's about damned time."

"Ellie Jane Weston." The admonishment came from a tall, slender, sixtyish woman with silvery hair and stern blue eyes who appeared in the entryway behind Ellie. "You watch your language."

"Sorry, Ma. Brady's home," Ellie announced to the woman.

"I heard. Why, I wouldn't be surprised if every

one of the surrounding counties heard.'' Claire Weston eyed her only son for a long moment, before her gaze softened. ''It's about damned time,'' she finally declared, moving past her daughter to pull her son into her arms. ''It's been much too long.''

''I wanted to come home sooner, but I didn't—''

''It doesn't matter.'' She shook her head. ''You're here now. That's all that matters.'' Another hug and she pulled away.

Surprisingly, her eyes glistened with tears and something shifted inside of Brady. While growing up, he'd seen his mother cry only once and that had been at his father's funeral. Claire Weston, as strong as the 150-year-old oak tree growing in the backyard, had buried relatives, seen her family through many trials, and not once had she lost control of her emotions, a character trait that no doubt pleased her father-in-law. Tears were for the weak, and there wasn't anything weak about the Westons.

One hundred years ago, Miles Weston had started Weston Boots all by himself. He'd hand-tooled leather from sunup to sundown, using little more than a make-shift tin shack out behind his barn as a workshop. He'd started something that generations after had continued. The Westons were hard workers, diligent, persistent, *strong*.

"It's good to see you," Brady said, giving his mother a warm smile.

"I hope this means what I think it means," she told him.

"That depends."

"I don't care what the old man says, you're staying."

"We'll see." He smiled and wiped at a stray tear gliding down her cheek. "You're looking as sexy as ever."

She sniffled and gathered her composure. "I see you've still got a fresh mouth."

"And you're still the prettiest woman in Cadillac." A loud cough and he turned toward his sister. "One of the prettiest women." Ellie rewarded him with a smile. "And speaking of pretty women, where are Brenda and Marsha?" Brenda was his oldest sister and Marsha the next to the oldest.

"Brenda's in Arizona for the next few weeks learning all about her uterus," Ellie said.

"What?"

"She and Marc are finally going to give in to Granddaddy's nagging and do the baby thing. But you know Brenda. She's a perpetual planner. Before she even thinks of going off the pill, she wants to know everything there is to know about conception and babies. She's at a convention given by Dr.

Something or Other who wrote that book *My Uterus, My Friend.* Marc's going to the workshops with her."

"And Marsha?"

"She's at a sales meeting in Chicago. She wants to expand the business, but Granddaddy isn't so sure. She's testing the waters with a few samples of next year's line of snakeskin boots. You should see the new rattlesnake—"

"I really don't want to talk business on an empty stomach," their mother cut in. "You," she said turning to Brady, "are just in time for lunch. I'll get Dorothy to set another plate and we'll catch up on old times. And then you two can talk about whatever you like."

"Yes, ma'am. I see she's still a slave driver," he told his sister.

"What do you expect? It runs in the family."

"Yes, but she married into the family."

"That's even worse. It's a double whammy. We're cursed."

"Lunch," Claire said as if keeping with her image. "Now."

Brady managed two steps before he heard his grandfather's voice drifting from the dining room.

"...need is a damned sheriff who knows the difference between a bull and a heifer. Why, John

Macintosh is as citified as they come and only on the lookout for his own interests and those old cronies over at city hall. Damned politicians..."

The voice, so rich and deep and familiar, sent a wave of doubt through Brady and he hesitated.

He'd envisioned this moment the entire trip from Dallas. He was about to face his past, his present, his future. *If* Zachariah Weston could find it in his heart to forget and forgive. Or at least forgive.

"He's still as salty as ever, but I can promise he won't bite."

"That's a matter of opinion," Ellie piped in behind them. "When I had my hair colored last month, he'd liked to have chewed me a new butthole."

"Ellie Mae Weston. I'll not have that kind of talk in this household."

"Sorry, Ma, but I can't help it if it's true."

"You colored your hair green. It's understandable he had issues with it. You represent Weston Boots. I wasn't too thrilled myself."

"I'm stuck behind a stack of accounting ledgers and a computer screen. No one even sees me. Besides, green hair was no cause to go and write me out of your will."

"I did no such thing and you know it." She pinned her youngest daughter with a stern glare.

"But I wouldn't go counting your chickens yet, young lady. There's still time, especially if you keep pushing me."

Ellie touched the now purple tufts of hair sticking up on her head. "It's just fashion, Ma."

"It's *purple,* for pity's sake." Another shake of her head and Claire Weston sighed. "I swear you're trying to send me into an early grave."

"Hey, I'm not stupid." Ellie winked at Brady. "Can't give her a chance to change the will, now, can I?"

"Ellie Mae Weston!"

"Sorry, Ma."

Claire shook her head and turned back to Brady. "Pay her no nevermind. Your grandfather is as ornery as ever, that's true. But he's missed you. We all have."

"I've missed you all, too."

"Now." She hooked her arm through his. "Let's go in and say hello." Before he could protest, she ushered him forward, steering him down the hall and into the dining room. "Look who's joining us for lunch," she announced as they walked into the room.

"If it's that freeloading Slim Cadbury from the VFW, just tell him to go find his own apple pie. I don't care how nice he is, he isn't getting so much as a whiff. Why, the man's only interested in you for your food, Claire. Don't I keep telling you that—'' The old man's words stumbled to a halt as his gaze lit on Brady.

Time seemed to stand still for Zachariah Brady Weston for the next several moments as he stared at his only grandson, his gaze as black, as unreadable, as Brady remembered.

His first instinct was to turn and run. He'd always felt that way whenever he'd been under his grandfather's inspection. Every Sunday morning before church. Every afternoon at the boot factory. Every Friday night after one of his high school hockey games.

And he'd always reacted the same. He'd simply stood his ground and waited for the criticism to come, praying for the approval. More often than not he'd received the first, but on occasion, the old man had smiled and congratulated him on a job well done.

This didn't seem to be one of those occasions.

Rather than dwell on the doubts raging inside him, Brady took the time to notice the changes eleven years had wrought.

His grandfather's hair had gone from a salt-and-pepper shade to snow-white. The lines around his eyes seemed deeper, the wrinkles etching his forehead more pronounced and plentiful. He looked older, yet his eyes were as blue and as bright as they'd always been. Brady knew then that eleven years might have aged the elder Weston on the surface but, deep down, he was the same man he'd been way back when.

Unease rolled through Brady and he had the urge to turn and walk away again. Now. Before he put his pride on the line and subjected himself to his grandfather's rejection—again.

Brady forced a deep breath and met the older man's penetrating stare. He wasn't going anywhere. He'd waited for this moment for much too long. Dreamt of it when his life had been less than perfect and he'd regretted leaving in the first place. He couldn't turn back now. He wasn't going to, no matter the outcome.

Brady's gaze clashed with blue eyes so much like his own and if he hadn't known better, he would have sworn he actually saw joy in the old man's eyes. The same joy he'd seen time and time again when he'd been younger, following his grandfather around the boot plant or the pasture or the barn.

Brady had always followed, at least when it came to his family. Among the rest of Cadillac, he'd been a leader, but at home he'd let others lead, content in knowing that one day he would have his chance to step up to the plate and bat.

He'd been a good, obedient grandson until he'd thrown it all away that one fateful day and gone against his family's wishes. All in the name of love. A no-no as far as Zachariah Weston had been concerned.

*"There ain't room in a man's life for both work and family. Take your daddy for instance. He tried to have it all and worked himself into an early grave. You've got plenty of time to have a wife and family. Now's the time for work. For focus,"* he'd said.

"Aren't you going to say something, Zach?" Claire prodded, disrupting Brady's thoughts. "Brady's come all this way to see us."

The man reached for his napkin and tucked it in at his neck. "When are we going to eat?" he asked Claire.

She planted her hands on her hips the way Brady remembered from his childhood. While she held the same values as her father-in-law, she'd never been quite as obedient as he'd wanted when it came to standing up for what she thought was right. And, of course, she'd distracted Brady's father at a time when he should have been focused on the company.

"Is that all you have to say?" Claire asked.

"What are we eating?"

Claire growled. "You're stubborn, you know that?"

"I'm hungry, that's what I am. Call it what you like."

She eyed him a few moments more. Then, as if she'd decided on a new approach, her expression softened and she smiled. "Doesn't Brady look good? Thanks to those Weston genes, of course."

Brady stood stock-still beneath his grandfather's disapproving gaze as the man swept him from head to toe. He knew what the elder Weston thought of his attire—the silk dress shirt. The expensive slacks. Yuppie, that's what Zachariah Weston was thinking. His only grandson had turned into a yuppie.

The sad truth was, he was right. Eleven years had taken their toll.

But no more, Brady vowed for the umpteenth time. He was shedding his image and getting back to his roots. His past. His *family*.

The old man's gaze dropped to the dusty cowboy boots Brady had unearthed the day before he'd left Dallas.

"Those are Weston boots," he told Claire, obviously intent on giving Brady the silent treatment.

"They're *my* boots." While Brady had inherited his sense of duty from his grandfather, he'd also inherited his mother's spunk. "You gave them to me, remember?"

"Tell this young man that, of course, I remember. I ain't that old." He eyed the boots again. "They're still Weston boots."

"And I'm a Weston."

Zachariah didn't say anything for a long moment. He simply stared and thought. Brady could practically see the wheels spinning as the old man decided his grandson's fate in those next few tense moments.

"Well, don't just stand there," the man finally barked at Claire. "Get the boy a seat. He's here. He might as well eat."

Brady let out the breath he hadn't even realized he'd been holding, and the tension eased. Zachariah Weston didn't eat with strangers. He only broke bread with friends, loved ones, *family*.

A warmth filled Brady as he slid into a nearby seat, followed by a swell of regret. Regret for all the lunches he'd missed. For the family he'd missed.

But he was home, and he was going to make up for lost time starting right now.

"DOROTHY REALLY OUTDID herself." Zachariah leaned back in his chair and puffed on his pipe. "Never had apples that tender."

"They were good," Brady commented, but his grandfather didn't so much as spare him a glance. He kept his gaze trained on his daughter-in-law.

"Ask him why he left Dallas."

"Why don't you ask him? He's sitting right in front of you."

"I don't belong there," Brady spoke up before his mother could give the old man a piece of her mind. And she would. Claire Weston had never had trouble standing up to her husband when he'd been alive and the same went for his ornery father. "I never did."

His gramps didn't say anything for a long moment. He simply puffed on his pipe and stared at Brady.

"Ask him what his plans are," he told his daughter-in-law.

"Listen, old man, I'm not your puppet—"

"I was thinking I might like to try my hands at making boots again," Brady cut in.

"Did you hear that?" Claire leveled a frown at Zachariah. "Or do you need to turn your hearing aid up?"

"I don't wear a hearing aid, little lady, and

you'd do well to remember who you're talking to." He waved his pipe at her. "I can't imagine he still knows anything about making boots or that he's ready to give it his all."

"Just like riding a horse," Brady said. "Once you've climbed into the saddle and taken a good ride, you never forget and I wouldn't give anything less."

"Horse riding," Claire paraphrased, obviously tiring of arguing with the old man. "You never forget and he's dedicated."

The old man nodded and puffed a few more times before a thoughtful look crept over his expression. "I could use an extra pair of hands down at the factory. Not for some frou-frou position, mind you." He motioned to Brady's silk shirt. "I've got Ellie running the office and she doesn't need a bit of help. She's a whiz with numbers and loves every minute."

"I'm not an accountant," Brady told his grandfather, who didn't so much as spare him a glance. "I'm an ad man." *Was* an ad man.

"Tell him I ain't got room for one of those either."

"Good." Brady spoke up before his mother could open her mouth. "Because that's not the type of position I'm interested in."

"It takes focus, not to mention he's liable to get his hands dirty," Granddaddy warned.

"Just the way I like them."

"We'll see," Zachariah said as he puffed on his pipe and gave his only grandson one long, slow look. "We surely will."

"THIS IS BULLSHIT," Ellie declared later that afternoon as she pulled her Jeep Wrangler into the parking lot and braked to a halt. "You should be in charge of operations instead of hammering soles onto a bunch of cowboy boots. *Hammering*, of all things. I can't believe he's starting you out at the bottom. You might as well be just another—"

"—guy off the street," he finished for her. "Right now, I am. He doesn't trust me and I can't say as I blame him."

"What?"

"I betrayed him."

"You stood up to him. There's a big difference."

"Not to him, and until I prove myself again, then this is the way it's going to be. Lots of hammering and lots of silence."

"And that's another thing. Have you ever seen anything so juvenile as him talking to you through other people? He's crazy. That's all I have to say.

And mean. And I have every intention of telling him so. Not that he'll listen to me either, but I'm going to do it anyway.''

"Let it go, Ellie. If putting me through my paces and giving me the silent treatment will make him feel better, then that's what I'll let him do.''

"You've got a college degree, for Pete's sake.''

"And he's got a lot of resentment towards me. He needs to vent.''

"So you're going to be his whipping boy until he comes to his senses, is that it?''

"I'll do what I have to do. I knew what I was facing when I left Dallas.'' And he'd been eager to get back anyway. To escape the daily grind and put the past eleven years behind him.

"But it's still not right,'' she persisted. "You shouldn't be doing something you hate. No one should.'' A faraway look crossed her eyes and Brady had the distinct impression that she'd died her hair green, then purple, not to make a fashion statement, but to make a personal one. Namely that she wasn't as happy hiding behind those ledger books as his grandfather apparently thought.

"Maybe not.'' But it felt right. Brady had worked in the hammering department as a teenager and he knew the work. What's more, he liked it. The heavy weight of the hammer in his hands and the scent of leather in his nostrils. "Trust me, I'm looking forward to every minute. You don't know how much I missed this place." He stared through the windshield at the large brown building that sat on the far edge of the Weston Ranch.

Once a barn, the structure had been expanded throughout the years and bricked over to accommodate the growing boot company. A small gravel parking lot sat to the right of the building. Brady trained his eyes on the patch of trees just beyond and glimpsed a large corral in the distance. He didn't need a closer look to know that the place stood empty. Gone were the animals that had once put muscle behind the large machinery used in the leather process when Brady had been a small boy. He'd been barely four when his grandfather had converted to the much cheaper and more convenient electricity. The massive tanning machines operated at the flick of a switch. Ovens that had once been fired up every morning by hand now had temperature knobs.

His grandfather had been determined to keep Weston Boots competitive in the ever-changing market place. Factories pumped out more and more and so the man had been hellbent on doing what he could to compete. And he'd succeeded. Somewhat.

The company was holding its own, but it wasn't moving. Ellie's books had indicated a steady profit over the past six years and while the numbers weren't dropping, they weren't increasing to represent the changing economy. The company needed a boost. He pushed the thought aside, however appealing. He wasn't an ad man. He made cowboy boots. End of story.

"Don't get me wrong." Ellie's voice pushed past his thoughts and drew his full attention. "I'm glad you're home. Damned glad. But after living in Dallas all these years, I wouldn't be surprised to see you go stir crazy over the next few days. This place is hardly the Exxon Towers."

"No," he agreed, "it's not even close." Which was the point exactly. The fading structure was completely opposite from the sixteen stories of steel and concrete he'd grown accustomed to. "Accustomed," as in tolerant. But he'd never developed a true liking for the skyscraper, much less the surrounding big city.

*This* he liked. The smell of grass. The sight of trees. The feel of the sun beating down on him, making sweat run in trickles from beneath the brim of his faded Resistol.

A smile tilted his lips as he climbed from the passenger seat and followed his sister toward the building. Familiarity rushed through him as he touched the rusted wagon wheel that hung on the front door of the building—the same wheel that had been hanging on the door since Weston Boots first opened back in the late 1800s.

"I keep telling Granddaddy to get rid of that," Ellie said as she came up behind him. "But you know better than anyone how stubborn he can be." She drew in a deep breath. "We're running with a skeleton crew since it's Saturday—Granddaddy's only day off—so you're not likely to get the real feel until the place is packed and all departments are up and operational. That'll be first thing Monday."

"That's okay. It'll give me a chance to get the feel of things again without worrying about slowing down production." He pushed open the door for his sister, then followed her inside.

"No problem, but do it fast because I've got a surprise planned for later."

"What surprise?"

"If I told you, then it wouldn't be a surprise, now, would it?" She smiled as if she held a big secret. "Let's just say, it's not every day the prodigal brother comes home. The occasion definitely calls for a celebration."

"As in a party?"

Excitement lit her eyes as she nodded. "As in an intimate party with the old gang."

He returned his sister's smile. "You never could keep a secret."

"How could I when you practically stuffed haystack needles under my fingernails to get me to talk?"

He grinned and let the door rock shut. Nostalgia rushed through him, along with a sense of peace and he simply stood there in the doorway, absorbing the sight and sound and smell of the place.

"What's wrong?" Ellie asked, her brow wrinkling as she studied him.

"Nothing," he said, sliding his arm around her as he guided her inside. "Everything's right. For the first time in a long time, everything's right."

"I'M AFRAID I'VE GOT bad news and good news," Merle, still clad in overalls and T-shirt, told him after Ellie dropped him off at the service station to check on his car later that afternoon.

"Give me the bad news first."

"I cain't exactly do that. It really is bad news *and* good news all rolled into one. See, Janie Gingrich—she's the lady that used to rent the room above the garage before she married Trent Mulberry—had this nasty crow that got loose and took up residence in the tree just in back of the shop."

"Is this the good news or the bad news?"

"Both, I told you. Bad news because the critter's been living in the tree behind the shop. Only comes out when he hears my wrecker pull up. Came squawking by when I pulled in with your sports car and pooped all over the hood. I shooed her away." He waved his rolled-up issue of *Popular Mechanics*. "But it was too late. She scratched the paint before I knew what had happened."

"And that's good news, too?"

"Sure enough. I'll have to wait until Monday to get the paint from Austin, but good because I'd have to have the car until then anyway so's I can take a look at that cracked engine block and look for any permanent damage. I know, I know," Merle said when Brady started to talk, "it's not in keeping with my twenty-four hour guarantee, but this being Saturday and all and Sunday not counting, it's technically only twenty-four work hours." He eyed his nephew. "You're not mad about the poop, are you?"

"Not if you've still got that room above the garage."

Merle grinned and fished in his pocket. "It's

yours,'' he declared as he handed over a slightly bent key. ''It ain't much, just a one-room with a kitchen, but it's clean. Maria sees to that.''

''That's good enough for me.'' Brady took the key and retrieved his bag from the backseat of his Porsche.

''Mighty pretty car,'' Merle said as he trailed his hand along the door. ''Minus the poop, of course.''

''Yeah, it is nice.'' Nice was an understatement. It was the best, like everything else in his life. Sally never would have settled for less. Even when they'd been dead broke, she would spend the last dollar to buy one gourmet cookie that lasted all of a few bites, rather than a loaf of bread to last them all week.

The dollar days had passed and he'd gone on to bring home more money, which she'd promptly spent. Always buying the best, from clothes to cars to fifty-dollar decorative handsoaps that he hadn't been allowed to use. They'd been for show like everything else in her life. Status had meant everything, and so she'd moved on when someone with more status had come along.

Thankfully, she'd finally done what he couldn't because of his damned conscience. She'd ended their marriage. Cut him loose. Sent him on his way so she could climb higher on the social ladder.

Or was that why she'd left?

*I need a real man who can satisfy me.*

He pushed aside the words as he headed up the stairs to the one-room efficiency. He wasn't dwelling on the past. He was living for the moment. For right now. And right now involved taking a shower so he could meet his younger sister and the rest of his old buddies for a much-needed drink.

"Look out, Cadillac. Here I come."

# 3

"I NEED a screaming orgasm in the worst way."

"You and me both," Eden told the woman who plopped down at the bar later that evening, a near empty glass in hand.

Dottie Abernathy was a regular Saturday-afternoon customer and one of the few who didn't give a fig about Eden's reputation.

Then again, Dottie had had her own reputation to contend with before she'd married the local fire chief and made a respectable woman of herself. Bib boobs—and Dottie had been blessed with two Double D's—equaled an even bigger reputation, and so the woman understood what Eden had had to endure. She was in her late forties with graying red hair and a die-hard makeup habit that made the town's only Avon lady the number-one-ranked salesperson in Texas. Dottie had a few too many gray hairs and her crow's feet were deepening, but in her prime she'd stirred her fair share of gossip.

"I know why I need one," Dottie said, taking

the very last sip of her drink. The woman was referring to the outrageously named beverage, while Eden had an entirely different orgasm on her mind. "James is at home planted in front of the TV and I'm here alone. But what's your excuse?"

Withdrawal. That's what had stirred Eden's hormones into a frenzy the moment she'd spotted Brady Weston. Sure, he was handsome and sexy, but he was still just a man. A walking Y chromosome. Nothing to get all excited about, unless the woman getting excited had been so busy the past six months working and worrying over the future and Jake Marlboro and what new stunt the slimeball was going to come up with to screw up her business that she'd completely neglected her personal life.

No wonder she'd been hot and bothered since walking into the Pink Cadillac after dropping Brady off at Merle's. She was deprived. Desperate. Due.

Yep, she was *definitely* due for a good, quality orgasm.

Not that she'd ever had anything close to a *screaming* one. Sure, she'd whimpered. She'd sighed. She'd even moaned a time or two. But no man had ever made her scream. Despite the rumors circulating around the small town.

Rumors. That summed up Eden's life to a T, at least from the tenth grade up. She was one great big rumor. Her past. Her present. Her future.

Rumor had it that she'd slept with the entire football team her sophomore year, and that she was presently sleeping with every elk over at the ledge, including Homer Jackson who, everyone in their right mind knew, preferred bulls to heifers any old day. As for the future? She would probably sleep her way through the city council, or maybe boff every police officer on the ten-man force.

Rumor. That's all it was, with the exception of one really cute elk Eden had met last New Year's Eve at the annual holiday party. They'd dated a few times and slept together once, and that had been the end of it. He'd been a horse trainer for one of the nearby ranches, and once breaking season had ended, he'd left for New Mexico and another ranch.

She'd moaned with him. Not so much because the sex had been great. Looking back, she could objectively qualify it as so-so. But she'd been coming off a long dry spell after her last fling nearly four years ago at a bartending convention in Austin, and even so-so had been an occasion for moaning.

But a bonafide *scream?* Not this girl. Not with

any of the handful of men she'd actually slept with, much less the hundreds that filled her make-believe résumé since Jake Marlboro had lied about her and made her the scarlet woman of Cadillac, Texas.

"Eden?" Dottie waved her empty glass. "Are you still with me?"

"Uh, yeah. Sorry. I guess I zoned out for a little while. It's been so hot out." She turned and twisted the air-conditioning knob a few notches cooler.

"You're telling me. Hit me again."

Eden had nothing against a woman quenching her thirst, but she wasn't in the habit of contributing to the delinquency of friends. Particularly when she sensed an underlying motivation propelling Dottie toward a second drink.

"Haven't you reached your one orgasm limit?"

Dottie Abernathy let out a pitiful sigh. "Usually, but I'm feeling *very* neglected today." She stared down at her empty glass. "Not that I really need the calories. Jerry's sure to run the other way if I pack on a beer belly."

Eden winked. "That's a screaming orgasm belly, and I can't imagine Jerry doing such a thing. He loves you."

"He loves me from February through July. It's August." At Eden's blank look, she added, "Preseason. I've dropped to number two on his priority list.'' She sighed. ''At least it's not number three. I don't drop that far until October when deer season opens. Right now, I'm going head-to-head with the Dallas Cowboys.'' She eyes the bowl of honey-roasted cashews sitting on the counter behind Eden. ''What about those? Those are healthier than an orgasm, right?''

''Definitely the good kind of fat,'' Eden told her as she grabbed the bowl and placed it in front of Dottie. ''And I won't have to drive you home.''

''Men,'' Dottie said around a mouthful of nuts. ''I'll never understand them.''

''Amen.'' Eden popped a cashew into her own mouth. She'd tried understanding them. When Jake Marlboro had taken the treasured gift of her virginity and turned it into a sleazy strip show, she'd tried to see the entire event through his eyes. Had she done something to make him think she was sleezy? Had she come on too strong? Too soon? Had she been deserving of his nasty rumors?

Hell, no. That's what she'd finally decided, after a lot of soul searching and years of heartache. The fine, upstanding citizens of Cadillac could see what they wanted to see—namely that Jake was a wealthy, enterprising member of the community and she was little better than a cow pattie stuck to the bottom of his boot.

As if she cared.

She'd stopped caring a long time ago about other people's perceptions—make that *mis*perceptions—when she'd finally come to terms with the fact that her first true love was nothing more than a lying, conceited, egotistical jerk.

Then and now.

Her gaze swept the nearly empty bar. *Empty* when she'd always been packed at this time of afternoon. Even Mitchell Wineberg who gathered with his cronies for Saturday-afternoon dominoes wasn't in his usual corner. He was over at the VFW, thanks to Jake who'd donated a twenty-seven-inch color TV to the rec room that put her small nineteen-inch black-and-white to shame. Who wanted to watch Pat Sajak and Vanna White in black and white when they could see that wheel spin in vivid technicolor? Not a one of them would give the Pink Cadillac a second glance thanks to Jake's latest contribution. If Eden wouldn't sell out, Jake would force her out by making the Pink Cadillac obsolete when it came to fun and entertainment.

Or so he thought.

She wasn't going down without a fight. She

didn't know what she was going to do, but it would be something foolproof. She wasn't selling the Pink Cadillac, no matter how much money he offered her.

Eden told herself that for the umpteenth time and turned her attention to Dottie and the bowl of cashews.

"...the Cowboys, of all teams," the woman was saying. "I could understand if he had me going head-to-head with the Packers. Now there's a decent football team. And cute. Why, they drafted a wide receiver with muscles out to here and a butt that begs to be pinched."

Dottie's comments stirred a vision of another very pinchable butt and Eden's attention shifted back to Brady and the picture he'd made standing on the side of the road, looking so hot and sweaty and sexy and...*hot*.

A twinge of longing shot through Eden and she reached for a handful of cashews.

Wait a second. Longing?

No way. Not when it came to a man. If she'd learned anything in her lifetime it was that men were a dime a dozen. Sure, there were those few good ones. Her father and Reverend Talbot and old Mr. Murphy over at the grocery store who climbed his apple tree out back every afternoon so his ailing wife could have fresh fruit with her lunch. Eden wasn't so jaded that she'd stopped believing in Mr. Right. He just wasn't lurking anywhere in Cadillac or the surrounding six counties.

But someday...

She dismissed the thought. Eden wasn't the type to sit around dreaming about the future. She made the best of the present and the matter at hand—which, right now, was her business and the only thing she longed for was a rush of customers. That would show Jake Marlboro that he couldn't win at everything. While he'd certainly gotten the best of her once, it wasn't going to happen again.

"These days, the Cowboys ain't worth the price of a hot dog at Texas stadium. But way back when they could make me sit up and take notice. Why, I remember when Jimmy Johnson was running the team..." Dottie droned on about the good old days and the nostalgia of the past as Eden poured herself a soda.

Nostalgia. That explained her reaction to Brady Weston. It wasn't so much that she was attracted to him now. No, she was remembering her attraction to him then.

The daydreams... All those times she'd sat in the bleachers and watched Brady throw a winning pass and fancied herself the head cheerleader and the object of his sexy all-star smile.

The fantasies... When she'd lounged on the bank of McKinney's Lake and watched Brady swing out over the lake in his best Tarzan imitation with the rest of his buddies. The rich kids. The haves. While Eden had sat on the opposite side with the have-nots, and pretended she was his Jane.

The reality... That one hot summer day when he'd had a flat and she'd given him a lift. In the close confines of her dad's beat-up pickup truck, with Brady so close and the heat so overwhelming, she'd come so close to living up to her reputation, sliding across the seat and kissing the devil out of Brady.

She'd wanted to, more than she'd ever wanted anything in her life. The feeling had been just as strong when they'd been on their "date." Throughout the night, Eden had wished he would ask her out for real. And she'd also wished he wouldn't be such a gentleman.

But that was in the past. Fond memories. A young girl's crazy infatuation with the sexiest boy in high school. Those days were over and she was all grown up now, and she didn't salivate over any man, no matter how handsome.

Besides, he wasn't *that* good-looking. Gone was

the clean-cut, freshly shaven golden boy who'd taken the Cadillac Texans to the state football championship not once, but twice. The years had added a hardness to his once soft brown eyes. He was older now, with tiny lines rimming his eyes and a roughness about him that came with years of hard living.

Not her type at all. Eden preferred pretty-boy Ricky Martin to the Marlboro man any day. Brady Weston was a little too different from the All-American who'd dominated her adolescent fantasies. He was too masculine, too sexy, and he was here—

Her thoughts slammed to a halt as she straightened and focused on him standing in the doorway. His gaze collided with hers and he smiled, and for five full seconds Eden actually forgot to breathe.

"Hey, Eden!" The greeting came from Brady's sister Ellie, who came up next to him. The woman waved and steered her brother into a nearby booth.

Eden had barely forced a calm breath, much less responded when the door swung open again. A group of men and women walked in and made a bee-line for Brady and his sister.

The past pulled her back as she remembered all the lunches spent staring across the school cafeteria. She'd sat with her friends while Brady had held court amid the A-crowd in the center of the lunch-room.

There were several beer bellies now and a few pairs of fake breasts, but otherwise the group could have been plucked from the yearbook pages as they smiled and laughed and piled into several booths surrounding Brady and his sister.

"Looks like tonight's going to be busy," Dottie said, drawing Eden away from her musings and back to the fact of the matter—she had customers.

Her gaze shifted to Brady, to his sexy smile and the handsome picture he made sitting there in a straw Resistol, faded jeans and a white T-shirt. Gone were the designer clothes and the preoccupied look from this afternoon. He'd transformed back into the good-natured, relaxed cowboy who'd smiled at her from the side of the road that day so long ago. The same cowboy she'd stared at day after day in her English class.

Only he hadn't stared back at her then, not the way he stared at her now.

The look he fixed on her was different. Older. Wiser. *Hungrier.* What's more, that looked called her forward. Beckoned to her. Along with a deep, sexy male voice.

"We'd like to order."

The prospect of getting close, of feeling his body

heat the way she had the other afternoon had an immediate effect on her. Heat rushed through her, making her nipples throb and her thighs ache, and for several long moments it was all she could do to simply breathe.

"I think they want to order." Dottie's voice finally drew her away from the sound of her own thundering heart, back to the present and the fact that her feet were still glued to the same spot, despite the fact that she had a booth full of much-needed customers.

Her first instinct was to call Kasey. Eden hadn't taken a break in several hours and the young woman could easily leave whatever chores she was doing out back to fill in for Eden out front. To *save* her.

The minute the thought hit, she forced it aside. What was *wrong* with her? She was bold and daring Eden Hallsey. She was the one who made men nervous, not the other way around. She made them sweat and want and *need*. Drawing in a deep breath, she gathered her courage and reached for her order pad.

Eden barely managed a few steps before Ellie called out, "Bring us some of your best champagne. We're celebrating. Brady's home!"

*Saved by the little sister.*

Relief swamped her and she turned before she could dwell on the feeling and the fact that she was actually nervous about approaching Brady Weston. She headed through the double doors that led past the rest rooms to the back room where she kept her stock.

She was *not* nervous.

She was pleased. Thrilled. Ecstatic. She had a dozen new customers and it was shaping up to be the most promising Saturday evening she'd seen in a very long time. All she had to do was ignore her ridiculous schoolgirl fantasies and concentrate on her business.

Sexy or not, Brady Weston was just a man. And men she could handle. She knew what they thought when they looked at her, what they wanted, what they expected, and the knowledge gave her an advantage.

That's what she told herself as she retrieved the champagne and pushed through the storage-room doorway. She'd barely taken two steps before she ran smack-dab into a wall of solid warmth.

One of the half dozen bottles she cradled in her arms slipped and hit the floor with a thunk and a roll.

"I'm sorry. I didn't see—" she started, the

words dying in her throat when her gaze shifted and collided with bright blue eyes.

"No harm done. I'm just glad nothing broke." Brady dropped to his knees and retrieved the wayward bottle.

"Wh-what are you doing back here?"

"Call of the wild."

The answer stirred several images. Of tangled sheets and sweaty bodies and *them*. Touching and kissing and...

She shook the thought and gathered her control. He was presumptuous, all right. But she hadn't expected anything different. He was a man. "You'll have to answer the call someplace else, buddy."

He arched an eyebrow and stared past her at the men's-room door. "You mean that isn't the men's room?"

Reality dawned and heat rushed to her cheeks. "You mean wild as in nature wild," she blurted. "I'm sorry. I thought you meant...I mean..."

"Thanks again for the ride this afternoon," he said, saving her from her own embarrassment.

"Glad to do it." She accepted the bottle from him, fighting back the heat that burned her cheeks. She'd misjudged him.

Maybe. Sure, she'd misread his comment, but that didn't mean that Brady Weston was different from the other men she ran into. She'd still caught him staring at her with that smoldering look in his eyes.

Like now.

"You haven't changed a bit," he told her.

"Really? And how would you know? You never even noticed me back in high school."

"Oh, I noticed you, all right. I couldn't help but notice."

"And what exactly did you notice?"

*Here it comes.* The cheesy comments about how pretty she was and how much he'd wanted to talk to her and go out with her and—

"You always smelled like peanuts."

Eden had heard enough pick-up lines to fill an entire volume, *Cheesy Comments that Desperate Men Make,* but this one actually surprised her. Still, original or not, it was just a line. A prelude to the kiss that was sure to come.

And he *was* going to kiss her. She could see it in his eyes, feel it in the tightness of his body as he leaned toward her.

Eden's heart pounded and she licked her lips in anticipation. *Here it comes…*

His mouth opened and his head dipped and he sniffed her.

Wait a second. Sniffed?

"Pistachios?" he murmured, his warm breath fanning her temple.

"Honey roasted cashews," she managed, doing her best to stifle the disappointment that rushed through her.

He leaned back and grinned. "That was my next guess. The champagne's getting warm," he said as he moved past her toward the restroom. "Thanks again."

Before Eden could take her next breath, he disappeared into the men's room and she was left staring at the closed door, her heart pounding and her lips tingling and her mind racing.

He'd sniffed her, of all things. No kiss. No attempt at a kiss. Not even a touch. Just a sniff. A *sniff*.

"Mitch," she called out, turning to walk back into the back storage room where her employee was stocking cases of Lonestar. "Take over the bar." She handed over the bottles, pulled off her apron and retreated into the kitchen.

Brady had just proven beyond a shadow of a doubt that he wasn't like the other men she came into contact with. he was different, one of a kind, and Eden wanted him.

For the first time in her life, she actually wanted

a man. She wanted to kiss him and touch him and talk to him, and the realization scared her.

Almost as much as it excited her.

HE WAS STUPID.

Stupid, stupid, *stupid.*

Eden had been practically begging for his kiss and he'd *sniffed* her, of all the crazy things.

What the hell was wrong with him?

The question echoed through his head for the entire evening as he talked and laughed and got reacquainted with his old crowd. But it was the answer that followed him down the street toward his room above the Gas-n-Go and crawled into bed with him much, much later.

"I need a man who can really satisfy me."

Satisfy. That's what it all came down to and, after eleven years of a not-so-satisfying marriage, Brady didn't know if he was up to the task. He wasn't, according to his ex-wife.

Then again, she couldn't see him right now. A quick glance down at the bulge in his jeans and he smiled.

And then he frowned. After all, having the equipment roaring and ready to go was different from actually doing the job. There were lots of guys out there who could get it up. It's what a man did with what he had that separated the stallions from the plow horses.

*Satisfaction.*

Did he have that something extra—be it know-how, an inbred sexuality, whatever—that would enable him to truly satisfy a woman? That special something that would make her call out his name in the middle of the night?

Forget call. He wanted a woman to scream for him.

But did he have it? Did he know what really turned a woman on?

Brady wasn't sure if it was the four beers coupled with the glass of champagne he'd chugged down at the Pink Cadillac, or the fact that he was half-exhausted and not thinking too clearly, or just a textbook case of insanity that made the answer suddenly obvious. Hell, it could have been all three. He didn't know. He just knew there was a solution to his problem.

He'd find a woman and satisfy her fifty ways 'til Sunday.

Then he would *know,* deep down in his soul, that his ex had been a gold digger like his family had claimed, and that he was still the same man he'd been when he'd walked away from Cadillac. Still a Weston. Still in control of his life and his destiny and his identity.

But it couldn't be just any woman. It had to be *the* woman that had haunted him so many nights when he'd been a naïve high school kid.

Eden Hallsey.

The name stirred a vision of her as she'd been tonight, staring up at him in the hallway, her lips plump and parted, desire gleaming in her eyes.

She was all woman. Hot. Sexy. Temporary.

His groin tightened and he shifted in the bed to make himself more comfortable. Yes, he was going to sleep with Eden Hallsey. And prove to himself, once and for all, that he was every bit a man.

# 4

---

"WAIT UNTIL YOU HEAR the hot news," Kasey
Montgomery announced as she waltzed into the
stockroom at the Pink Cadillac for Sunday-
morning inventory.

Eden glanced at her watch. Make that Sunday-
afternoon inventory. "You're late."

"I think my Timex stopped." She slapped her
oversized tote down on the floor and sat down on
a crate of Lonestar.

"You don't wear a Timex," Eden pointed out.
"Or any watch for that matter."

The blonde glanced at her bare wrist as if seeing
it for the first time. "Wow. No wonder I'm late."
Kasey popped the tab on her Diet Coke and cast
an excited gaze on Eden. "So there I was coming
out of the TG&Y—they just got a special order of
the Vampin' Red lipstick I've been lusting over
ever since I saw it in last month's issue of
Cosmo—and who do you think I saw?"

"Laurie Mitchell with her very own tube of

Vampin' Red.'' Laurie was the town's reigning beauty queen and Kasey's arch enemy since she'd taken her Miss Cadillac crown and her reputation as the local beauty authority. The comment drew the expected frown and Eden smiled. Since she couldn't bring herself to dock Kasey's pay for her notorious tardiness—she and Kasey had been friends since sixth grade when they'd shared a pack of Bubblicious gum during gym, followed by a stint in detention for getting caught—the least she could do was yank the girl's chain every once in a while. ''Can you pass me that jar of swizzle sticks?''

''For your information, Laurie wouldn't know her Vampin' Red from her Seductive Scarlett if her poor, pathetic, bleached blond life depended on it.'' Kasey handed over the container of multicolored sticks and her frown disappeared as excitement crept back into her expression. ''I saw Anita Kingsbury,'' she announced. ''That's who.''

''Anita practically lives at the TG&Y. She does needlepoint and it's the only store that stocks the thread. That's not hot news.''

''Of course it's not. Anita was carrying the news. She'd just been to the Piggly Wiggly where she'd just run into Janie Tremaine who'd just been to Mabel's for a permanent.''

"Janie traded in her straight hair for a permanent?"

"And a haircut, but that's not the point. See, while Janie was having the extra small rollers done on her crown, she overheard Sarah Waltman who'd just come in for a bilevel trim with shagged bangs."

"Sarah's going with shagged bangs?"

"Wild, isn't it? But that's not the point either."

"Then what *is* the point?"

"Guess who Sarah ran into before she arrived at Mabel's?" Before Eden could answer, Kasey rushed on, "*Him,* that's who."

"That tells me a lot. Do you know how many *hims* there are in this town?"

"Approximately .75 for every female," Kasey replied. "And you're not listening. I didn't say him. I said *him.*"

"Now that clears up the mystery. Can you turn around and give me a pretzel count?"

"I can't believe you've forgotten." Kasey reached for a jar of pretzels instead and popped the lid. "Fifth period," she said around a mouthful. "Mrs. Jasmine's sophomore English class."

Eden penciled in the pretzel figures. "You're eating up all my profit."

"It's just a handful." She put the lid back on.

"Just add them to my bill. So guess who's back in town?"

"Mrs. Jasmine."

"No, silly." Kasey grabbed the clipboard and reached around Eden for a bag of popcorn. "It's Brady Weston. You know Brady with-the-cutest-butt-at-Cadillac-High Weston? Don't tell me you've forgotten the highlight of our pathetic sophomore lives?"

If only.

The trouble was, she remembered all too well. How cute he'd looked walking down the hall in his tight jeans and letterman's jacket. How sexy he'd seemed every time his full lips had curled into a grin. How irresistible he'd been standing on the side of the road that unbearably hot summer day.

Eden pushed the thought aside. Okay, so she was attracted to him. She was also a grown-up rather than a hormone-driven teenage girl. She'd perfected her control over the past ten years.

"You *do* remember him?" Kasey persisted, opening the bag and dishing a handful of the butter-flavored snack into her mouth.

"Vaguely."

"And Laurie and I are the best of buddies."

"Okay, so I remember him. That goes on your

tab,'' she told Kasey as the girl reached for another
handful of popcorn.

"Him and his butt.''

"Remembering someone usually entails all parts
of them.''

"Man, that was an ultra-fine butt. Go on,'' Kasey prodded. "I know you remember. Just admit
it. Confession is good for the soul.''

"Okay, so he has an ultra-fine butt.''

"*Has,* as in present tense?'' Kasey folded up the
half-eaten bag of popcorn and studied her.
"You're holding out on me.''

"Maybe I've seen his butt for myself.'' When
Kasey looked ready to burst with curiosity, Eden
added, "Yesterday I picked him up on the road
outside of town and gave him a lift.''

"And you didn't tell me?''

"This is the first time I've seen you since yesterday.''

"That's worthy of a phone call. So?'' she prodded after a long moment when Eden didn't say
anything.

"So what?''

"So what does he look like now?''

"Would you believe a receding hairline and a
pot belly?''

"Brady Weston? Not on your life. C'mon and spill it."

"The same." At Kasey's doubtful look, she gave in to the smile playing at her lips. "Better."

"I knew it!" Excitement flashed in the girl's eyes as she wiggled her eyebrows. "Does he still sound the same? All deep and sexy?"

*I know who you are.* Brady's words echoed in Eden's ears and heat shimmered along her nerve endings. "Deeper and sexier."

Kasey let out a whoop. "I knew it. And his smell?" A dreamy look crept over her expression. "Does he still smell as good as he did back in English?"

Eden's nostrils flared at the memory of Brady sitting next to her and stirring her senses with his clean, musky scent. "Better."

"I knew it. It's the age thing. Brady is like a classic '69 Mustang. Granted, way back when it was still a hot car. But now…it's mega-hot. A classic. Maturity makes all the difference. The added years make Brady look better. Sound better. Even smell better."

"And here I thought my cologne was responsible for that last one." The deep voice slid into Eden's ears and shimmered over her nerve endings. The hair on her arms stood straight up and heat rushed to her cheeks as she turned to find Brady standing in the storage-room doorway.

"My, my, if it isn't Mr. Brady Weston." Kasey slid off the crate and stood, tugging at her blouse as if she were fourteen again, back in Miss Jasmine's class. "Why, it's been ages since I've seen you."

"Much too long," Brady agreed, but his gaze wasn't on Kasey. His attention rested solely on Eden.

She wanted to look away, to break the connection between them and regain her composure. The trouble was, she knew it was a useless effort. She'd never had it together where Brady was concerned. He was different. He'd always been different. From the moment he'd pushed all rumor aside and planted that soft, sweet kiss on her cheek after their first and last date.

Brady was the sort of man dreams were made of. The gallant white knight. And time seemed to have changed little.

Unfortunately.

"So how long have you been standing there?"

"Long enough to be thankful that I don't have a receding hairline and a pot belly."

"That long, huh?" She shook her head and tried

to ignore the strange sense of self-consciousness he stirred.

*If only.*

"I guess you heard us carrying on about you, then," Kasey said. "Man, you were something."

"Were, meaning past tense." He grinned. "Thanks a lot."

"Oh, it's not just the past. The present is pretty fine, as well."

"Kasey has no shame," Eden said when Brady chuckled.

"Shame'll get you nowhere on a Friday night. A girl has to go after what she wants. Speaking of which," she grabbed another bag of popcorn and headed for the doorway, "I need lunch."

"That makes ten bucks," Eden told her as the girl scooted by.

"You should be the one paying me," Kasey whispered. "Most women would kill for a chance to be alone with such a cute hunk."

But Eden wasn't most women and Brady Weston wasn't just any hunk. He was the *only* hunk she'd ever really been attracted to. She'd gone out with guys and kissed more than her fair share, but none that she'd really *wanted* to kiss. She'd kissed and petted because it had been expected of her, but with Brady she'd felt the need clear to her bones.

The winning ticket had been a godsend, or so she'd thought. One date. The chance to finally, *finally* satisfy her curiosity and kiss him. There'd been no doubt in her mind that it would happen. Brady was just a guy, after all, and all guys reacted to her—or rather, her *reputation*—in exactly the same way. They expected to score and wasted little time with preliminaries. She'd had no doubt that things would be the same with Brady, but the notion hadn't upset her. She'd wanted him too badly and so she'd been ready. Excited. A first for Eden Hallsey where boys were concerned.

She'd had another first that night, however. She'd learned that all men were not hormone-driven, egotistical low-lifes. There were a few white knights out there, namely, one handsome, luscious football team captain who'd treated her like a lady the entire evening and given her a chaste good-night kiss on her forehead.

She'd been disappointed and thrilled at the same time. A deadly mix that had her daydreaming the rest of her high school career about things Eden Hallsey had never dared to dream before.

Or since.

Things like marriage and babies and happily-ever-afters.

But Brady had been too much one of a kind.

While he'd renewed her faith in men, she'd yet to meet another man like him.

"I never knew there was a Brady cheering section," he told her once they were alone.

She shrugged and did her best to look nonchalant. "Maybe there wasn't. Maybe I knew you were there all along and Kasey and I were just carrying on for your benefit."

Something passed over his expression the moment she voiced the possibility. A strange look of insecurity, but then it was gone and his grin slid back into place. "So you remember my butt, do you?"

She tried to sound nonchalant. "Vaguely."

He grinned. "I remember your butt, too. And," he added, his gaze sweeping her from head to toe, "all the rest."

Her heart pounded at the prospect. "Really? And here I never thought you gave me a second glance."

"Oh, I gave you a second look. And a third. I just couldn't do any more back then."

Because he'd had a girlfriend. A beautiful, popular, possessive girlfriend, and while Eden had heard many rumors that things weren't so great in paradise, Brady had never let on otherwise. He'd been loyal, and Eden had liked him all the more because of it.

She still liked him, if the thunder of her heart was any indication.

"I…" She licked her lips and tried for a calm voice. "I—I think something's wrong with the air conditioner. It's really hot in here."

"Amen to that," he said. His eyes fired a brighter blue and she knew he wasn't referring to the air surrounding them, but the heat flowing between them. "But it's not your air unit, darlin'. I think it's you. And me."

"I don't know what you mean." The statement was so unlike her. With any other man she would have flirted rather than played the coy virgin. She wasn't a virgin, and she certainly wasn't coy. Not since that day when she'd offered herself to Jake the Butthead Marlboro.

But this was different. He was different.

"There's chemistry between us," Brady pointed out. "There's always been chemistry, but it's stronger now. Too strong to ignore." He leaned closer and ran his fingertip along her jawline. "You feel it, don't you?"

She nodded.

"We should do something about it."

She nodded, her heart pounding faster. This was

it. The moment she'd dreamt of all through high school. Brady Weston was actually going to ask her out on a real date.

"Sleep with me."

The request sent a burst of disappointment through her, followed by a rush of excitement unlike anything she'd ever felt before. All those years of holding him up on a pedestal suddenly seemed so useless. He was no different from the other men she'd met. His request proved as much.

Now she knew the truth. Her head did, that is. But her body, with its fluttering heart and sweaty palms and shaky knees, had yet to get the message.

"The attraction between us is too powerful to ignore, darlin'. What do you say? Just for one week?" he continued, a sexy grin on his lips.

Eden pondered the problem. She still wanted this man despite the fact that he'd clearly proven himself to be just as much of a jerk as every other man. She could see only one solution.

Once she slept with him and turned Brady from a dream man into a plain, ordinary, flesh-and-blood male, she would stop responding like some silly, naive teenager. His image would be totally shot and he would be out of her system, her curiosity satisfied once and for all.

"Yes."

Yes?

Was she totally nuts?

*Hell, no. You're Eden Hallsey. Cadillac's most notorious bad girl, and you're going to do what any bad girl would do with such a hot, sexy man. You're going to have sex with him.*

That's what Eden told herself. The trouble was, this was Brady Weston. The one man Eden had lusted after since puberty. The only man who hadn't lusted back.

Until now.

It seemed as if Brady had turned out to be just another one of the guys wowed by her bad girl image. Far from the gentleman she'd initially thought.

The realization left a bitter taste in her mouth but, at the same time, she couldn't suppress the excitement that pounded through her at the prospect of next Saturday night—the first in a week of nights to remember.

They'd made all the arrangements of a traditional date—Saturday night, the Pink Cadillac, eight o'clock—but the evening to follow would be anything but.

*Cheap, tawdry and degrading.*

Those were the adjectives that should have come to mind. They'd eliminated even the tiniest bit of romance by planning a night of sex as if it were a trip to the dentist.

But over the next few days as the weekend approached, it was *sexy, exciting and empowering* that kept her heart beating fast and her blood racing.

With his wicked smiles and brilliant blue eyes, Brady was the epitomy of *sexy.*

For a woman whose sex life had been practically nonexistent, the prospect of being with such a man was *exciting.* Like a child about to open a present she'd been eyeing under the Christmas tree, she was finally going to know what it felt like to really kiss the man of her dreams. But it was also *empowering* because, despite the intense disappointment she felt at discovering Brady wasn't the white knight she'd always envisioned, there was still something oddly liberating about doing away with all the silly cat-and-mouse games that most men and women played. They both knew what they wanted and they were adult enough to cut right to the chase. No flowers and candy. No empty promises. Just a night of hot, wild sex to sate the lust burning between them.

*Yes!*

# 5

"YOU'RE UP AWFUL EARLY this morning." The comment came from Zeke Masters, an old high school hockey buddy and the newest addition, besides Brady, to the Weston Boots hammering department. "I'm only here this early because once 7:00 a.m. rolls around, we run out of hot water over at Mrs. McGuire's," Zeke continued.

Mrs. McGuire ran the only boarding house in town, which was where Zeke had been living since a very public breakup with his wife of ten years. She'd taken the house over on Main and his job at her parents' horse ranch, while Zeke had ended up with the clothes on his back and a pop-up tent he'd been using prior to the hellacious rain that had blown the canvas away six weeks ago. He'd had to resort to renting a room, which meant he needed money, which explained his presence at Weston Boots. "Cain't stand the cold on my bare back, so I'm up and out 'afore the crack of dawn. What about you?"

"Thought I'd get a head start on things." That, and catch his grandfather who was notorious for beating the workers to their spots. The man lived for sunup and Brady was determined that whatever Zachariah Weston liked, he was going to give him.

He eyed the white pastry bag and steaming foam cup sitting on his work bench.

"Is that what I think it is?" Zeke asked, his nostrils flaring.

"White crème-filled donuts with chocolate sprinkles fresh from Gentry's Bakery." His grandfather's all-time favorite.

"Sure does smell good."

"That's what I'm counting on."

But the crème-filled donuts didn't live up to his expectations ten minutes later when his grandfather walked into the building.

"Good morning," Brady said as the old man walked by. Other than the slight flare of the man's nostrils, he gave no indication that he was even aware of Brady's presence, much less interested in pastries.

So much for an edge.

Brady grabbed the bag of donuts and handed them to Zeke. "Knock yourself out."

"Thanks," the man said a moment later around a mouthful of donut.

"It's nothing." Unfortunately. But Brady wasn't giving up. He'd known that winning his grandfather's favor back wouldn't be easy, but he was determined to try. Today was just the beginning.

"I hate Mondays," Ellie groused later that morning as she walked into the Weston Boots office, a cup of cappuccino in one hand and a donut in the other.

Brady pulled off one of his gloves and wiped the sweat from his brow. "Think of it this way. Monday is the beginning of the week. A fresh start."

She frowned. "I should have known it."

"What?"

"With all that smiling you've been doing. All the grins and the winks, and all without benefit of caffeine." She eyed him and nodded. "Yep, it's a sure thing."

"What?"

"Dallas turned you into one of those bright-eyed and bubbly morning-a-holics."

Actually, that transformation had come about just a few short days ago when Brady Weston had rolled back into Cadillac to reclaim his former life. Before that he'd been like every other big city suit—consumed by his work. He'd spent his evenings, his weekends and most holidays at the office. And all to maintain the lifestyle that Sally had grown accustomed to. He'd worked his ass off to please her. To live up to his responsibilities. To honor the commitment he'd made when he'd said "I do."

*She's not your kind.* His grandfather's words echoed in his head the way they had so many times over the past ten years, but Brady forced it aside. He wasn't dwelling on the past. He'd made his mistakes and learned from them. Today was a new beginning. The first day of the rest of his life right here in Cadillac.

He grinned and raised the blind. Sunlight streamed into the office and Ellie shielded her eyes. "You're trying to kill me, aren't you?"

"Now why would I do that to my favorite sister?"

"You're still mad because I told Katy Milner that you wanted to give her a hickey."

"Actually, little sis, I'm glad you told Katy. She stopped playing hard to get and came after me." He grabbed her donut, took a bite and winked. "Don't work too hard."

Ellie snatched back what was left of her breakfast and growled. "I'd say the same to you, but I know you're not going to listen. You're determined to make the rest of us look bad.''

"I'm just glad to be back. To be doing something I actually like.''

"I wish I could say the same.'' Ellie's words followed Brady out the door and down the hall to the staircase that led to the second-floor administrative offices. He'd started to wonder if his presence was to blame for his little sister's perpetual foul mood. After all, she'd had their grandfather all to herself for the past ten years and now she had to share him. But there was something else going on, something deeper, and Brady once again speculated that, perhaps, Ellie wasn't happy with her life.

"Hey there, son.'' His grandfather's voice sounded behind him and killed any more exploration of the subject. "Ready to tackle a full day's production?''

The question drew a full grin. The old man had actually asked him a direct question.

At least, that's what Brady thought until he found his grandfather staring past him at Zeke, who still had a speck of white crème at the corner of his mouth.

"Why, yes, sir. I'm always ready.''

"He are you were here early today. I like that.''

"I like to get a jump on my work."

"Or a jump into the shower," Brady grumbled. Not that he was being a bad sport. He'd known winning his grandfather's favor back wouldn't be easy, but he was determined to try.

So determined that he showed up the next morning with his grandfather's favorite pancakes and sausages from the Turtle Diner over on North Street.

The old bull at least did more than sniff. He actually glanced at the foam box before ignoring Brady's good-morning, congratulating Zeke on his punctuality and heading for his office.

"Man, are you sure you don't want some of this?" Zeke asked when Brady handed him the breakfast.

"I've lost my appetite."

For food, that is. But he was still hungry for something else. For someone else. For, although his days were filled with thoughts of winning over his grandfather, his nights were overflowed with fantasies of Eden.

The thought drew a vision of her, her lips slick and pouty from his kiss. They'd just shared one kiss. But come Saturday night there would be more. More touches. More kisses. *More.*

His heart pounded at the thought. But as the

week progressed, the nights long and sleepless and the days filled with work, his excitement turned to anxiety. After all, he was going to sleep with the woman. Time to find out the truth.

*I need a real man.*

"Damn, boy. What's wrong with you?"

"Nothing," Brady replied before he realized that his grandfather's question wasn't directed at him. As if he could expect anything different.

"Zeke," he said to the young man fighting with the branding iron, "you got to get a better grip than that if you want the brand to be deep enough to last, and everybody knows a real pair of Western boots has a brand that lasts."

"Sorry, sir, but I used to break horses, not brand them. I'm afraid this is new to me."

"Now, Granddaddy, stop grousing at Zeke. Everybody who's ever picked up a brand knows it takes time to get it right," Ellie said as she waltzed past, box in hand, and handed out paychecks, the late Friday-afternoon ritual.

"New? Why, he's been here a full two weeks. I was branding on my first day."

"Which is why you're the boss," Ellie told him as she handed over the box of checks and walked over to Zeke. "It's really not that hard," she told the young man. "Just think of it as branding a heifer, but a lot less trouble. After all, the boot's not going to whine or put up a fight. There's zero chance you'll get kicked. See—'' She took the branding iron in one hand and a brand-new boot fresh from the tanner in her other. ''Hold it just like this for about five seconds and, presto, you've got a custom-designed, one-of-a-kind Weston boot.''

''Thanks, Miss Ellie,'' Zeke said after she demonstrated a second and then a third time before handing him the branding iron.

''Anytime.'' She winked before turning and retrieving the paycheck box.

''I need those account reports by this afternoon,'' their grandfather told her.

''I'm on it.''

''And last month's invoices.''

''Why didn't you tell me that earlier? I've still got to finish up the balance sheets for the previous month and it's already noon.''

He slid his arm around her shoulder and gave her an affectionate squeeze. ''Guess you'll have to order in for the three of us. Zeke and I are going to take a look at that old tanning machine that keeps cooking the leather. I like to show all my new guys all the equipment, even the malfunctioning kind.''

New, as in Brady. Only Zachariah Weston wasn't treating him like the other newbies. He was ignoring him. Punishing him.

Brady clamped his lips together and turned back to the hammer and leather at his fingertips.

"I checked the timer on that old machine last week," he told Zeke as he ushered him down the hall, "and it seems to me—"

"It ain't the timer," Ellie said as she followed.

"Sure it is."

"But I tested it myself and—"

"Give Murray over at the Pig-n-Pit a call, would ya, darlin'? And order us up a couple of double rib burgers with onion rings. It'll be my treat since Zeke, here, has been so punctual every morning. Got to reward good work habits."

"But I..." She caught her bottom lip and chewed for a long second before shaking her head. "No problem."

"That's my girl." He patted her shoulder and a smile spread across her face. But the expression didn't quite touch her eyes and Brady got the feeling that she wasn't nearly as pleased with their grandfather's comment as she wanted him to think. "And you'll have the reports by this afternoon."

"Never a doubt in my mind, honey. Now you run along and let us get to work."

Work. The one and only thing that helped Brady get through the rest of his day. He could focus his attention on something constructive rather than fret over his grandfather's coldness, not to mention the coming weekend.

And he was fretting.

What had started out as excitement had quickly morphed into full-blown anxiety as the moment of truth approached.

*I need a real man who can satisfy me.*

His ex-wife's parting words haunted him for the next few days, feeding his anxiety until Friday night arrived and Brady found himself questioning his decision.

Did he really think he could satisfy a woman like Eden Hallsey?

He knew her reputation. She wasn't some wet-behind-the-ears virgin who would cling to him. She was a real woman. A sexy-as-all-get-out woman who wouldn't be content with clumsy kisses or a mediocre performance in bed. For Eden he would have to go the extra mile.

The trouble was, after eleven years in an un-happy marriage, Brady wasn't sure if he knew what that *extra mile* entailed.

But he intended to find out.

With that vow in mind, he pulled out of the

parking lot of Weston Boots late that Friday evening and headed into town for some reinforcements.

BRADY STARED through his windshield at the red tin building located one street over from the main strip through town. White trim accented the door and window shutters and gave the place a barn look. Of course, it *had* been a barn way back when Cecil Montgomery had used it to house his milk cows before selling out to Lulu Kenner—the oldest, meanest math teacher to ever smack a hand while working out an algebraic equation. Thanks to a double order of chili fries that had sent her husband Jeb to his death and a nice, fat insurance check, Lulu had given up her ruler, taken an early retirement and gone into business for herself.

Brady glanced up at the red neon sign glittering in the window. Miss Lulu's Video World.

Hey, it wasn't Lookin' for Love, the adult store located a few blocks over from his office back in Dallas, but it would have to do. He'd seen the blazing red neon sign on more than one occasion, but he'd never had a mind to pay a personal visit. He'd been too busy working himself from dusk 'til dawn, living up to his responsibilities to worry about his carnal knowledge.

Or lack of.

He closed his mind to the negative thought and climbed out of his pick-up. Coming home wasn't about regret. It was about living. Today. Tomorrow.

Tomorrow night.

Boots crunched gravel, the sound mingling with the buzz of crickets as he walked to the entrance. A bell tinkled, announcing his arrival, and Brady soon found himself in the new release section of Miss Lulu's.

"Can I help you?" The voice drew him around and Brady found himself staring at a young teen, a Cadillac High football jersey pulled tight across his young chest. A straw cowboy hat sat perched atop his head while a toothpick wiggled at one corner of his mouth. "If you want *Coyote Ugly,* there's only one copy and we're fresh out. We're always fresh out since I finally talked Granny into ordering the danged thing in the first place." He grinned. "Said there wasn't much of a story line, but then I convinced her it weren't the story line that was going to sell the blasted thing and we were in business. Now I do all the ordering. And the clerking when I finish practice. So what can I do you for? You looking for a particular title?"

"Not really."

"Something featuring a certain actor. Me, I watch everything with Demi Moore. She's hot."

"I'm not too particular. I just need something that a woman would like."

"You mean a chick flick? One of those tear-jerker movies? I got just the thing. *Steel Magnolias*. It's got all this female bonding stuff and—"

"Not that kind of a chick flick. Something more...romantic."

"Sure thing. *Ghost*. It's an older movie, but the chicks really go for it. It's like a psychological, undying love sort of thing and—"

"I mean *romantic* romantic."

"Sure thing. Right over there is *Gone with the Wind*. You can't get more—"

"Sexy. I need sexy."

"Well, there's always *American Gigolo*. I can't see it myself, but my girl says Richard Gere's about as sexy as they—"

"Sex," Brady blurted. "I need sex." He drew in a deep breath. "Do you have anything that's romantic and physical with a female slant?"

A light bulb seemed to go off in the young man's head and he smiled. "Sure, man. I've got just the thing."

Several minutes later, Brady found himself walking out of Miss Lulu's with a bagful of videos, including *9 1/2 Weeks,* an erotic thriller guaranteed to give him some pointers on really satisfying a woman.

After eleven years in a not-so-satisfying marriage, Brady needed all the help he could get.

"SO I TOLD HIM, it's either me or Rudy T."

"I thought Jim was into football," Eden told the twenty-something blonde sitting at the bar, nursing a beer late Saturday afternoon. Trina McWilliams had married her college sweetheart, Big Jim, a little over six months ago. The entire town figured them for the perfect couple. Whenever Big Jim was out plowing his field, Trina would be perched up on the tractor right next to him.

"Jim *is* into football."

"Well, I hate to tell you, but Rudy T is the head coach for the Houston Rockets." At Trina's blank look, Eden added, "They're a basketball team."

Reality seemed to dawn and Trina shook her head. "No wonder he looked at me as if I'd grown a third eye. I'm not really into sports." She shook her head. "Maybe marrying Jim was a big mistake. After all, what do we really have in common?"

"It's only been a few months. Give it some time."

"And it'll only get worse," Dottie Abernathy

said as she slid into her usual seat at the bar and requested her screaming orgasm. "Now it's football," she told Trina as she reached for a nearby bowl of popcorn. "Next year he'll be into baseball. Then there's basketball. And hockey. And just wait until hunting season." Dottie rolled her eyes. "When it's us or a big buck, darlin', guess who's plumb out of luck?"

Trina's face seemed to brighten. "Big Jim doesn't like to hunt. He's more into fishing."

"A buck or a bass, it makes no nevermind. The end result is the same. Zero time together."

"Don't listen to her," Eden said as she replaced Trina's empty beer bottle with an ice-cold Coke. "She's married to one of the nicest men in the county."

"Nice has nothing to do with it." Dottie turned to Trina. "I want attentive."

"Me, too. I mean, Big Jim is as sweet as a moon pie, but when the TV is on, I might as well not even exist."

Eden filled a bowl with honey-roasted cashews and slid it across the countertop toward Dottie. With the way she was already going on about her husband, she deserved to indulge tonight. "It's not full of testosterone, but maybe this will make you feel better." Eden turned her attention to her third and last customer. "Hey there, Grace. You okay with that soda?"

"Sure thing, sugar. But I sure could use some more of this popcorn." Her gaze never wavered from the television set perched in the far corner of the bar. Gracie McVie was one of the oldest residents of Cadillac and a die-hard court TV fan. Since the old folks' home out on the highway had hired a new social director who was also a fanatical dieter, the TV room had turned into a workout gym filled with back-to-back *Sweatin' with the Oldies* videos.

Gracie was too old to sweat, or so she'd told Eden the first day she'd walked through the front door and asked if Eden had a television. She hadn't had one back then, but she'd pulled her own from her apartment above the bar and hooked it up on a shelf in the far corner. Gracie had been forever grateful and had come in every Saturday since.

"Judge Jackie's about to give the heave-ho to that there seamstress for goofing on the plaintiff's wedding dress the day of the wedding. Imagine that. The day *of.* Why, if someone had goofed on my dress the day I married my dear, sweet Bernie—God rest his soul—I would've let loose a couple of rounds of buckshot and asked questions later. Of course, that was before my arthritis set in.'' She flexed her fingers. "It's hell getting old.''

"You're not old,'' Eden started, but Gracie had already waved her into silence.

"The judge is about to deliver his verdict.''

Eden was about to turn and head back to Trina and Dottie when she heard the voice behind her.

"Kind of slow for a Saturday night, isn't it?''

She tried to calm the sudden pounding of her heart. "Actually, this is the usual. The Pink Cadillac isn't the hot spot it used to be.''

"Since when?'' Brady asked as he reached the bar.

"Since Jake Marlboro decided he wanted to buy me out,'' she told him, noting how potently masculine he looked in his soft cotton shirt and Wranglers.

"I never would've had Jake figured for the bar owner type.''

"He isn't. He wants the Pink Cadillac and every other business on this block so that he can put up a MegaMart.''

He nodded. "My uncle mentioned that. I never pictured him owning a department store.''

"He doesn't own them. He just builds them. Mega hired him to site out the best location and construct store number two hundred twenty-seven.''

"And you got lucky."

"It's not luck. This bar has been in my family for years and it's staying in the family as long as I have anything to say about it." The trouble was, with business declining, Eden wasn't sure how much longer she would have something to say about it. Her savings would only last so long. After that, suppliers would stop supplying if the bills weren't being paid and then...

She forced the thought aside and turned her attention to Brady. Her nostrils flared and the hair on her arms stood straight up. "Did you come here to talk about my business?"

"I didn't come here to talk at all. Are you ready?"

This was it. Her chance to back out. To give in to the doubts racing through her mind and preserve the dream she'd nursed for so many years.

The trouble was, Brady had already killed that dream when he'd propositioned her. So there was no turning back.

Insecurity rushed through her, feeding her anger. Brady shouldn't make her feel so...self-conscious. He *wouldn't*. Not after tonight. Not after her body finally understood what her brain had known since the beginning of the week—that Brady Weston was just like any other man. Nothing special. Certainly not the shining white knight she remembered from high school. His propositioning her had colored the picture. Following through with it would shatter the entire thing and Eden could go back to thinking about her bar and forget all about the man who'd rolled back into town and turned her thoughts upside down.

"Let's go."

# 6

"WHAT ARE WE DOING HERE?"

Brady glanced from Eden to the grocery store where they'd pulled up. "I thought you might be hungry."

"I'm not," she stated, stiffly holding the flowers he'd handed to her when they'd reached the car.

"Well, I am." He started to climb out.

"But I thought we'd just cut right to the chase. I mean, you didn't say anything about us eating together."

"I didn't say anything about us not eating together. I just need to pick up a few things. Why so jumpy?"

"I'm not jumpy." She was clingy. The truth hit her as she glanced down to see her white-knuckled grip on the flowers. Taking a deep breath, she forced her fingers to relax. "I'm just not one for wasting time."

"It won't be a waste. I can promise you that

much,'' he said before disappearing inside the store.

Eden spent the next ten minutes doing her best to relax. Not an easy task with his scent swimming around her, teasing her nostrils, stealing inside her head. Why did he have to smell so good? Or look so good? Or be even nicer than she remembered?

Good-looking and arrogant, she could have handled. While confident, Brady wasn't the least bit full of himself. If she hadn't known better, she would have sworn she'd sensed a moment's hesitation when he'd climbed out of the car. As if he, too, was nervous.

Crazy. *He'd* propositioned *her,* after all. A woman was the last thing that would cause Brady Weston to be nervous, particularly Eden herself. Men had been many things around her—arrogant, insincere, flirty—but none had ever been nervous. Except Mikey over at the diner. But he was fifteen, with a face full of acne and a body full of raging hormones.

Brady Weston was a grown man. A handsome, sexy, grown man and she was just plain, old Eden Hallsey who'd sat behind him in English and lusted after him along with the entire adolescent female population.

''You must be really hungry,'' Eden commented

when he deposited a bag full of groceries on the seat between them.

"You can bet on it, sugar." His eyes glittered as they locked with hers and she knew he was talking about more than dinner. The crazy notion that he might actually be nervous about their interlude faded in the smoldering depths of his eyes.

The line begged for a comeback, but the only thing she managed was a weak, "That's nice," as they pulled out of the parking lot and headed down the main strip through town.

Thankfully, the drive to his garage apartment was blessedly quick. Otherwise, Eden felt certain she would have died of lack of oxygen. As she climbed from the cab, still clutching the flowers, she drew in a deep, lifesaving breath and tried to slow her pounding heart.

It wasn't the close confines, she decided as he ushered her up the stairs. They were out in the open and she still couldn't get enough air. It was the quiet. The unnerving quiet filled with nothing except the buzz of crickets and the thunder of her own heart.

"So this is where you live?" she asked once he'd kicked the door of the apartment shut behind them.

"For now." He deposited the sack of groceries on the sink and started to unpack.

Eden glanced around and noticed the squares of white cardboard littering the nearby sofa. She didn't mean to be nosy, but she desperately needed to be distracted from listening to her heart hammer in her chest.

"What are these things?" she asked, picking one up and studying the drawing of an old cowboy boot.

"Nothing. I've just been playing with a few ideas to beef up business."

"Your granddaddy has you working on advertising?"

Brady shook his head and Eden could have sworn she saw a look of pure longing on his face. "I'm working production. I *like* working production. This is just something I'm playing around with." He pulled a carton of ice cream from the bag. "But I'd rather play with you." His eyes gleamed. "What do you like? Chocolate or vanilla ice cream?"

"Chocolate, but I'm really not hungry." Her gaze swept the one-room efficiency, from the small kitchen to the leather sofa to the bed visible just beyond an open doorway. The place was small, but expensively decorated despite its location. Then again, she expected nothing less from the Westons. Even when they roughed it, they had style.

"Nice clock," she said as her gaze lit on a glittering chrome hubcab hanging on a nearby wall.

"Merle made it." He held up two jars. "You like chocolate or caramel syrup?"

"Caramel." her gaze went to the row of framed photos lining the wall. Each image depicted a group of children sporting the same uniforms. "These are the T-ball teams Merle has sponsored?"

"Yep."

"They're nice. I sponsor a team, too," she added.
Now, why had she said that? Because they were about to do the deed and she suddenly had the strange urge to get to know him. To share something about herself.

"Yeah, the Houston Astros, pint-sized edition," she continued. "I've sponsored them for the past eight years.

"I didn't see the team banner at the bar. Don't all sponsors have banners?"

"The league president, Conrad Phillips, doesn't like the fact the kids are sponsored by a bar. And I agree. I do sell alcohol, after all."

"And so does the Longhorn Steakhouse, but they have a banner."

"It's okay. Conrad's never really liked me, not since I turned him down for a date several years back."

"But he's been married ten years."

"I know." Eden studied the pictures again. "These are really nice. So...have you settled things with your grandfather?"

"Nut preferences. It's cashews, right? And just what do you know about the situation with my grandfather?"

"Yes to the cashews, and I know what everyone else knows. That you left and he got mad."

He took the flowers from her hands and placed them in some water. "He got more than mad. He disowned me."

"I know. I'm sorry."

"So am I, but I don't blame him. He had every right."

"You were only eighteen. Just a kid, and kids make mistakes."

"True, but a man's gotta do what a man's gotta do."

The comment hung between them for a few moments as he unloaded the rest of the groceries and Eden glanced around the near empty apartment.

"So this is your sofa? It's nice."

"Thanks."

"And your TV. It's nice, too."

"Thanks again."

"And I really like this lamp." Even as she stared at the base, also made from a giant hubcap, she couldn't believe the words that were coming out of her mouth. She'd never been into small talk. Neither had she ever nursed a pounding heart or tried to calm a racing pulse or fought for every breath.

Then again, this was Brady Weston. *The* Brady Weston.

"Look, can we just get to it? We agreed to sex, so there's no reason for all this small talk. I know you, you know me. We know what we want."

"Almost." He held up two small crates. "Strawberries or blueberries?"

"For the last time, I'm not hungry."

A slow grin spread across his face and a smoldering light lit his eyes. "Then let's see what we can do about that."

"WHAT ARE YOU DOING?" Eden blurted as Brady stepped across his kitchen, a satin blindfold in hand.

"It's called foreplay." He circled and came up

behind her. The hard wall of his chest kissed her shoulder blades. "You do want to play, don't you, darlin'?"

"Yes, but I was thinking more along the lines of a little kissing, some heavy petting. I don't see—" She stopped abruptly when his arms came up from behind and his palm brushed her cheek. Electricity skimmed through her body as two strong fingertips pressed against her lips.

"You don't need to see," he murmured. "You just need to feel." Before she could protest, his hand fell away and she felt the cool glide of silk against her skin. "As for the kissing and petting...I plan to pet you until you purr like a kitten. Make no mistake about that."

"I've never done anything like this," she blurted, a zing of panic rushing through her as the silk blocked out the light. With her sight gone, her other senses took control and became sharper in those next few seconds. Her nostrils flared with the aroma of warm, husky male. Her skin prickled from the heat of his body. Her ears seemed to tingle as they tuned in to the deep, husky murmur of his voice.

"Then this is a first for both of us."

Her heart thundered at the thought before common sense intruded. She fought for a calming breath. "I mean, I have," she rushed on, determined to take back her previous naive statement. Granted, it was true, but he didn't know that. No one did, and Eden intended to keep things that way. She had a reputation to uphold, after all. "Done this, that is. It's just, I didn't expect it. You said sex. Just sex. So I assumed this would be pretty straightforward. No frills. Just the basics." She knew she was rattling, but damned if she could help herself. Not when he smelled so good and felt so warm. "The bare bones. The nuts and bolts—" The words died on her tongue as something cool pressed to her lips. The scent of chocolate filled her nostrils and she realized it was one of the fudge truffles she'd seen him pull from the grocery sack.

"Let's see if you can do something else with that beautiful mouth of yours besides talk." His voice, so rich and deep, stirred her even more than the decadent aroma wafting through her nose. "If I didn't know better, I'd say you were nervous."

But he knew better. The whole town did. She was Eden Hallsey, bad girl extraordinaire. A woman who'd been around the block and then some, or so most people thought. What she wanted the entire town to think.

Everyone except Brady Weston.

The minute the thought pushed its way in, she

pushed it right back out. Brady was no different. He was every man she'd ever slept with—the few and far between—and every man who'd ever wanted to sleep with her. Nothing special.

And so Eden gathered her precious control and did what she did best. She put on her I-know-all-the-ropes persona and stuffed that small insecure part of herself down deep where it belonged. "I can do plenty with this mouth," she murmured in her most sultry voice. Her lips parted and she sank her teeth into the sweet confection, focusing on the burst of flavor rather than the strange fluttering of her heart.

This had nothing to do with her heart. It was all about satisfying her body and proving to herself once and for all that Brady Weston was just a man. Tonight would be exactly what they'd agreed upon....

"Just sex," she murmured to herself as she took another bite.

*Just* sex?

The thought stuck in his head as he watched her mouth work at the truffle. Was she crazy? Tonight was about more than a little no-frills mattress dancing. Much more. It was about great sex. Stupendous sex. The best of her life. So Brady spent the next few hours recreating his favorite scene from last night's erotic movie.

He'd picked what he'd dubbed the cherry scene, in which Mickey Rourke and Kim Basinger had sat in front of an open refrigerator and engaged in a uniquely delicious form of foreplay. With her eyes closed, Kim had sat dutifully in front of Mickey while he'd fed her everything from cherries to honey. The scene hadn't featured the sex act itself, but rather the buildup. Mickey had been intent on stirring all of Kim's senses, on truly turning her on.

Exactly what Brady wanted to do for Eden.

He succeeded over the next hour. She'd smiled quizzically when he'd told her about renting the video, but he'd also seen her hands tremble as she reached blindly for another spoonful of chocolate mousse. Her ripe nipples pressed against her T-shirt as he trailed ice down her chin and the slope of her neck. Her bottom lip quivered as she opened her mouth for a trickle of honey.

She had great lips, so full and pouty and kissable. It had taken all his willpower back in high school not to kiss her that night she'd won the date with him. But he hadn't wanted to be just every other guy in her eyes.

He'd wanted her to see him differently, as more

than just a conquest, though the notion hadn't sounded so distasteful. Particularly when she'd stared at him with all that young hunger in her eyes as he'd walked her to her door.

"You'll never know how much I wanted to kiss you that night. I wanted it so bad."

"Right." The incredulous look on her face almost made him smile. Almost, but he was too aroused, too intent, too eager to see if her nipples tasted as ripe as they looked beneath her thin tank top. The incredulity faded into curiosity. "You *really* wanted to kiss me?"

"Darlin', every guy in school wanted to kiss you. I was no exception."

She frowned and, for a split second, Brady had the distinct feeling that he'd said the wrong thing. But then her mouth tilted and she smiled, and the notion faded in the sudden burst of heat that shot through his body.

He moved to feed her another cherry, but she caught his hand. A few swift tugs behind her head and the blindfold fell away.

"May be if you're nice to me," she told him as she tossed the slip of silk to the side, "I'll give you that kiss now."

"That's not going to work."

"You're not going to be nice to me?"

"I've already been nice, and I'm not going to settle for a kiss after all this effort." He popped a cherry into his mouth and swallowed. "I want more, darlin'. I want you." And then he did what he'd been wanting to do since the moment he'd rolled back into town and Eden Hallsey had offered him a ride.

He picked her up and took her to bed.

WHILE THE PAST HOUR had passed with excruciating slowness, the next few moments were a dizzying blur. One moment Eden was sitting on Brady's kitchen floor and the next she was sinking down on the edge of his bed.

She watched, her lips parted, her breathing shallow, as Brady stripped in front of her. When he pulled off his shirt, her mouth grew dry at the sight of hard, smooth planes of his wide chest. When his hands went to his fly, her breath stopped completely. She had the barest glimpse of white cotton before he drew her to her feet and grasped the edge of her T-shirt. He held her gaze for one charged moment before pulling it over her head, swiftly and expertly. She wanted to step back, to take a good long look at his body, but she burned too fiercely for him. When his hands reached for the waistband of her jeans, a small voice in her head urged him faster, faster. He slid her button free and urged her zipper down. Cool air swept over her legs as he pushed down her jeans, leaving her in only bra and panties. He urged her down onto the bed and followed, his hard body covering the length of hers. The sudden sensation of heated skin against skin made her gasp.

Before she could draw in her next, ragged breath, he captured her lips with his own in a kiss that was even better than she'd anticipated. Hotter. Wetter. A moan worked its way up her throat and her lips parted for him. His tongue slid against hers, coaxing and hot, a fierce contrast to the coolness of the cherries she'd eaten just moments before. Sensation overwhelmed her and Eden closed her eyes, reveling in the flood of heat.

His fingertips slid toward the clasp of her bra and sanity zapped her. She caught his hand an inch shy and shook her head. "I like it on. It's sexy."

"It's in the way."

"Not really," she mumbled, glancing down at the dark tip of one nipple peeking up between the lace.

"I can see your point." He dipped his head, catching the ripe peak between his lips. His tongue lapped at the sensitive bud and her panic faded in a rush of heat.

He trailed his hand down her side, hooked his thumb in the edge of her panties and dragged the lace down until it pulled free and she lay naked beneath him. Almost. She still had on her bra and Eden intended to keep it that way.

Brady obliged her. He was too focused on other things, particularly the triangle of curls at the base of her thighs. His fingers ruffled the hair and slid along the dampness between her legs.

Her entire body seemed more alive than ever before in those next few moments. She felt *everything*. The rasp of his chest hair against her lace-covered nipples. The glide of his big toe down the inside of her calf as he shifted his position and nudged her legs apart. The pulse of his now condom-covered erection as it settled in the damp heat between her legs.

The past hour had, indeed, stirred her hunger and brought her body to throbbing awareness. She was on fire and each touch made her burn hotter, brighter.

Dipping his head, he kissed her again, rubbing his erection against her sensitive slick folds. Back and forth. Again and again.

She arched against him, every muscle in her body taut. Her breath caught on a sob as he pushed the head of his penis just a fraction inside her. Just enough to tease, to tantalize, to send a burst of feeling through her and push her close. So very close...

Through the haze of pleasure, she found him staring down at her, his eyes dark and smoldering as he watched. Meeting his gaze, she felt an intense jolt of awareness at the intimacy of this moment, this act, with a man she'd only ever fantasized about before. In that overwhelming moment, Eden did what any desperate woman would have done. She tilted her hips just so, drawing him deeper despite his obvious efforts at restraint.

He muttered a curse before giving in to her demanding body and plunging deep. His eyes closed and relief flooded her, followed by a burst of heat as he again plunged deep. So deliciously deep...

She wrapped her legs around his waist, holding on as he shoved his hands beneath her bottom and tilted her, driving deeper, stronger, pushing her closer to the brink until she could take no more.

Her orgasm crashed over her like a tidal wave, consuming her, turning her inside out and upside down. It was fierce. Intense. Mind-blowing. She barely managed to catch the cry that rolled up her throat.

But she did.

Old habits died hard and Eden had been holding

herself back, hiding behind a cool, seductive wall for much too long to stop now, even in the face of such delicious heat.

Because of the heat. It was too fierce. Too intense. Too...unexpected.

The realization stayed with her for the next few heart-pounding moments, as Brady drove deep one final time. That was the only time he broke the eye contact between them. As if he couldn't help himself, his lids shut and his back arched. Every tendon in his neck went taut as he groaned, long and low and deep.

Eden fought back the urge to touch his face, to trace the curve of his cheekbone, to feel the heat of his skin against her palm. Instead, she concentrated on her own body, on slowing the spasms that still rocked her.

He collapsed on top of her, his head resting against the curve of her shoulder, his lips pressed to the furious beat of her pulse, and it was over.

*Over.*

So why did she feel the need to do it all again? To feel the delicious pleasure? To give him the same pleasure again?

Eden closed her eyes as the truth crystalized in her brain. She'd anticipated a good orgasm. After all, he was so sexy and hot and so...Brady. She couldn't imagine anything less with the boy-turned-man who'd haunted her thoughts for so many years. But this... *this* went beyond a great release.

She wanted to jump. Shout. Laugh. Cry.

Worse, she wanted to throw her arms around him and beg him for another. And another.

The notion sent a burst of panic through her, and she did what any self-respecting bad girl would have done at that moment. She scrambled across the bed and reached for her clothes.

"Where are you going?"

"It's late," she managed in her calmest, coolest voice. She *was* calm and cool. And in control. And now was no different from any of the other sexual experiences she'd had in her past. They were finished, and so she was leaving.

"It's only midnight."

"Sorry, but I'm always in bed by midnight." Just as the words left her mouth, she felt his fingers encircle her wrist. A strong but gentle tug, and she found herself tumbling backward onto the bed.

"Then you're right on schedule, darlin'." His grin was slow and easy and heart-stopping. Heat rushed to her cheeks.

Great. Now she was blushing. First she'd stammered. Then she'd trembled. Now she was blushing, of all things.

She definitely needed to get out of here.

"*My* bed," she clarified.

"Lead the way, darlin'. I'm game again if you are."

"About that..." She crawled from beneath him and reached for her clothes. Blushing? She was *not* blushing, and she wasn't crawling back beneath the covers as she desperately wanted to. This was no different from any other sexual liaison. *He* was no different, even if he did touch her just so and kiss her until her toes curled and her hands trembled and... "I really have to get out of here."

"What about our date?"

"Tonight was hardly a date. It was an agreement. We agreed to sleep together. Mission accomplished."

"I thought we could get a bite to eat. I don't know about you, but I'm starving."

"I had dinner earlier."

"Then we'll have dessert." He quirked an eyebrow at her and grinned. "You don't have to run off. I won't bite. Unless you want me to, that is."

His words stirred a vision of him over her, kissing his way down the curve of her neck, nibbling the slope of her breast, licking the tip of her nipple...

The urge to jump back into the bed nearly overwhelmed her and panic rushed through her, sending her scrambling for her shoes. "Look," she said as she pulled on her boots, "it's nothing personal, but let's not make more out of this than it really was."

"And what exactly was it?"

Earth-shattering. Mind-blowing. *Romantic.* "Nice," she finally murmured, determined to get a grip on the small voice inside her that kept insisting otherwise.

*Any* man.

His grin died and his eyes narrowed. "Nice, huh?"

"Very nice. But now it's back to the real world. We've done the lust thing and now I really need to get over to the bar and help Kasey. She's probably swamped. Saturday's our busiest night, after all."

*Dream on, sister.*

"I thought you were going home to bed."

"I am. I mean, I was. I mean..." Great. She was stammering again. It's just, he smelled so good and looked so good, so dark and tanned sprawled there against the pale yellow sheets. Heat rushed through her body and her thighs tingled. She wanted another touch. And another kiss. And—

*It's over.*

"I am going home to bed," she managed as she snatched up her purse and made a bee-line for the door. "After I go to the bar." She reached for the doorknob. "I'll see you around."

"You can sure-as-shootin' bet on that, darlin'."

"I THOUGHT YOU HAD A DATE tonight," Kasey said when Eden walked into the bar ten minutes later.

"It wasn't a date. We just got together to talk over old times."

"I s that what they're calling it now?"

Eden shot Kasey a frown. "What's that supposed to mean?"

"Nothing. It was a joke. Since when did you get so touchy?"

Since Brady Weston had rolled back into her life and made her feel so nervous and anxious and...just *feel*. Something Eden hadn't allowed herself since she'd run from Jake's house crying the night she'd lost her virginity. She'd buried her feelings from then on, hiding behind her cool persona. But Brady shook the image and drew her feelings to the surface. He stirred her so fiercely that she couldn't bury the feelings anymore.

At least until tonight. But now that they'd done the deed, she'd gotten him out of her system. Her infatuation with him was over and done with. No more thinking and dreaming and seeing himself as anything other than the flesh-and-blood man that he was. No way was she going to keep trembling or hoping or dreaming. And no way did she want to do *it* again. Even if he had talked about a whole week.

"We might as well go ahead and close up," Kasey said, her gaze sweeping the empty bar. A familiar sight since Jake had set about using his strong-arm tactics to persuade the town that the Pink Cadillac was best left alone.

Strong-arm as in monetary incentives. Jake wasn't man enough to put any muscle into his threats. He simply bought his way around Cadillac, providing the bingo hall with a new speaker system in exchange for extended hours that cut into Eden's business and kept the Senior Singles playing double and triple cards rather than playing darts and nursing sodas in Eden's back room.

"You go on ahead. I think I'll get a headstart on tomorrow's inventory." Because the last thing Eden wanted to do was go home and climb into an empty bed. Heck, she didn't even want to *see* a bed. Not with her body still on fire. Still alive and wanting and—

*You're doing it again.*

Yep, inventory was what she needed, all right.

She locked up behind Kasey and headed toward the stockroom. Picking up her clipboard, she made her way toward the pantry and the twenty-odd jars of maraschino cherries.

A very vivid of image of Brady popped into her mind. His gaze dark and intense as he fed her a piece of the ripe succulent fruit. Her nipples pebbled at the remembrance and her blood rushed and the need to turn and bolt for his apartment nearly overwhelmed her.

She flicked the light switch off and plopped the clipboard onto the counter.

On second thought, inventory could wait until tomorrow.

# 7

*NICE?*

What kind of word was *nice?*

Brady pulled on his jeans and walked into the kitchen a good half hour after Eden left, a half hour he'd spent thinking and remembering and doing his damnedest to figure out what had happened.

Where was the screaming? The begging? The noise that follows supreme, earth-shattering sex? Hell, he would have settled for a smile of satisfaction, *anything* other than the passive look on her face as she'd donned her clothing and left him to question his manhood.

He sank down onto the sofa, a beer in hand. He popped the tab and downed a long swallow. *Nice* described a sunny Saturday afternoon or the pitter-patter of rain on a barn roof. The term didn't come close to touching the past two hours spent with Eden. He'd had sex before, but never had it been so hot, so intense, so damned terrific.

Then again, that was his opinion. Not hers.

*Nice.*

Had he failed to push her hot buttons?

The question bothered him all of five seconds, until he remembered the flush that had crept across her silky skin, the desire that had flashed in her eyes. Her body had milked his in a mesmerizing rhythm that had made him come harder and heavier than ever before, and his gut told him it had been the same for her.

She'd been turned on, all right. Hell, she'd been on fire. But, for whatever reason, she'd been dead set on controlling the flames. She'd concealed her pleasure on purpose, pushed it away just the way she'd pushed his hands away when he'd tried to remove the last stitch of her clothing—that lacy wisp of a black bra that had revealed a helluva lot more than it had covered.

*I like it. It's sexy.*

No doubt it was sexy, but Brady couldn't help but think there was more to it than that. She'd been too nervous when her fingers had grasped his. Too desperate when he'd toyed with the clasp of her bra. Too *scared.*

Eden Hallsey, bonafide bad girl and the sexiest woman he'd ever had the pleasure of touching, had actually been frightened of him.

Or herself.

The notion reminded him of the bashful, bright-eyed girl he'd known back in tenth grade, the girl she'd been before that Monday morning that changed everything. Eden had looked stricken and distant. And during the lunch hour, Brady had discovered why. According to Jake Marlboro, Eden had stripped for him *and* his entire baseball team. *Hardly.* Brady hadn't believed it then and he didn't believe it now. Yep, Eden was scared, but she needed to face her fear. And he was just the one to help her.

He got to his feet and walked over to the bag he'd brought home from the video store. While Eden might be of a mind that they were finished, he wasn't nearly done.

He pulled out another video and popped it into the VCR. Tonight had just been the warm-up. Brady was armed and ready for more, and he wasn't about to stop until she was back in his bed, completely naked, out of control and conscious of nothing—her insecurity, her anxiety, her fear—*nothing* save the heat that burned between them.

"COME AND SHARE your misery." Kasey's eyes lifted from the neon pink flyer. "I don't know much about advertising, but this doesn't exactly make the Pink Cadillac sound like the happening place to be on a Saturday night."

"The book I'm reading says to play off emotion and that's what I'm doing. I'm thinking, if Dottie and Trina—both football widows—like to come in to eat snacks, toss down a few brews and share war stories, some of the other women in town might want to join in also. See, these ladies aren't out to have a good time. They're interested in a sympathetic ear. A little friendly advice. Some understanding. That's what this flyer is all about. It calls to those lonely hearts in need of kinship, and that's what the Pink Cadillac is all about."

"Please don't tell me you're going to sing the theme from *Cheers* right now. After the night I had—" Kasey touched her head "—I don't think I could take it."

Eden couldn't stifle her grin. "Actually, I thought we could do a few verses of 'Kumbaya.'"

"You're trying to torture me, aren't you?"

"The hangover is doing that. I'm just trying to make you see that you don't have to compete with Laura Winchell on *everything*. Who cares if she can drink six hurricanes and still recite her ABC's? You don't have to follow suit."

"It wasn't as if I had anything better to do. *I*

didn't have a date with the hottest cowboy in Cadillac.''

"For the last time, it wasn't a date, and Brady Weston isn't a cowboy.'' Once upon a time he'd been the classic hero wearing the white Stetson and riding the white horse, but no more. He'd changed, despite the fact that he'd given her flowers and gone to all the trouble of renting a sexy video just to turn her on.

It had all been part of the game. The seduction.

The thing of it was, no man had ever gone to so much trouble to seduce Eden. Because of her reputation, men assumed she was like a light switch. One flick of a button and she was blazing hot. No muss. No fuss. No foreplay.

Certainly not three hours of it.

So? The end result had been the same. Sex. Granted, it had been outstanding sex, but the big S nonetheless. And now it was over and done with.

"Are you okay?" Kasey's voice pushed into her thoughts. "You look flushed.''

"It's hot in here.''

"We're in the refrigerator.''

"It's still hot in here.''

"It's sixty degrees.''

"It's hot. Would you stop changing the subject. When are you going to learn that you don't have to drink seven hurricanes to prove your superiority?''

"It was seven and a quarter, and it's the principle of the thing. Laura thinks she's so much better than me. She always has.''

"That's just her opinion.''

"Her and her dozen or so friends down at the Cut-n-Curl.''

"It shouldn't matter what those old biddies think.''

Kasey's eyebrows lifted. "Excuse me. This from the woman who puts her slinkiest dress on to go to church just so she can set those very same biddie's tongues to wagging?''

"That's different. It's not that I care what anyone thinks. I don't care, which is why I dress the way I want to.'' At Kasey's skeptical gaze, Eden rushed on. "But we're not talking about me. I'm not nursing a throbbing head and a queasy stomach.''

"The queasiness passed. I'm in full-blown nausea as we speak.''

"Go home and get some sleep.''

"But I can't leave you here all by yourself,'' Kasey protested, even as she abandoned her clipboard and reached for her purse.

"I think I can make it.''

"You're sure? Because all you have to do is say the word."

"Go."

A smile split Kasey's face. "That's the word I was hoping you'd say." Then she turned serious. "But just so you know, I would be the first to stay if you absolutely, positively, unequivocally needed me."

Eden arched an eyebrow. "Unequivocally? Are you and Laura taking an expanded language course?"

"Three nights a week at the community college." She started for the door. "Speaking of which, I'll need off early tomorrow night."

"How early?"

"Early enough for a full manicure. Laura practically lives in a French set."

Eden wondered briefly what it would be like to worry so much over something so superficial.

She'd never had the luxury. Her problems had always been real—not enough money, enough food, enough class.

That had been a contributing factor to Jake's rejection and betrayal. She'd been the wrong girl for him and so he hadn't taken her feelings seriously.

But she'd been serious. For those heart-pounding five minutes when she'd bared all, she'd been deadly serious. And scared. And hopeful.

No more. She was a grown woman and she knew the score. Namely, the haves didn't belong with the have-nots. Sure, it happened in movies. She was still a die-hard *Pretty Woman* fan. But real life? Eden had spent too many years with a reputation she hadn't earned, and all because she'd been from the wrong side of town. Jake would never had spread rumors about Mitzi Carmichael, the only child of city councilman Buford Carmichael and heir to the Double C—one of the largest purebred horse ranches in the country—even if Mitzi had done it with the Cadillac Wolverines' entire defensive line, and all in the same night. An incident that wasn't hearsay, but the God's honest truth. Eden had seen for herself when she'd walked into the back bedroom in search of an extra bathroom at one of Myra Jackson's infamous after-game parties.

Eden had seen it, all right, and the guys involved had even bragged about it, but no one had truly believed it because Mitzi was the product of good breeding and old money. Not the sort of girl to do something so outlandish.

But Eden? She was just the sort. Her parent s were gone now—both killed in a car accident years ago—but before that—her mother had served beers for a living while her father had poured them. Neither had ever set foot in church except on special occasions. They'd incited a fair share of gossip themselves when they'd been young, particularly since they'd lived together for several years before ever tying the knot.

They'd been the talk of the town way back when, and their daughter had inherited the title.

But while her parents hadn't been Ozzie and Harriet, they had loved one another, and they'd loved Eden. She hadn't had the best of everything, but she'd had all the basics. Food. Clothes. A warm bed in a clean house. Unfortunately that house had been located on the wrong side of Kendall Creek, and so Eden was an easy target for gossip, the sort that drew a man's attention. She was the outcast not even worthy of sponsor recognition for a local T-ball team.

And when it came to Brady Weston, she'd best keep that in mind. A pang of regret went through her—a feeling she quickly squashed. The last thing she wanted to feel was regret. Relief. Now there was an appropriate emotion. They'd done the deed, her curiosity had been satisfied, her drought ended, and now she could concentrate on her business.

Unfortunately, she'd felt anything but relieved

when she'd climbed into her bed late last night after closing up the bar. She'd tossed and she'd turned and she'd remembered.

The way he'd touched her, kissed her, cried out her name when he'd reached his climax. The way he'd stared at her when she'd reached hers.

As if he'd been waiting. Expecting.

She forced the thought aside. It didn't matter what Brady Weston had thought at that moment because *he* didn't matter.

One night.

And that night was now over.

She grasped that thought and turned her attention to the jars of salted peanuts lining one of the shelves. There was inventory to be taken and a bar to be cleaned. Eden spent the rest of the afternoon taking care of both.

It was well past sundown before she finally set her clipboard aside and removed her apron. Exhaustion tugged at her muscles and she smiled. The more exhaustion she felt, the better her chances of getting a solid, good night's sleep—

The thought crashed to a halt as the lights flicked off and darkness swallowed her up.

"Stupid lights," she muttered as she felt her way down the aisle, past several large shelves. Another step and she stubbed her toe. Pain rushed up her leg and pierced her brain and she sucked in a breath. A few more steps and she reached the cabinets at the far end of the room. She reached blindly inside the cabinet and felt for the flashlight. Her fingers closed around the familiar shape and a few seconds later a single beam sliced through the darkness. Eden was about to search for a spare bulb when the flashlight beam hit the light switch and she realized it was in the off position.

She closed the cabinet door and moved to the switch. A flick of her finger and brightness cracked open the darkness. Her heart pounded faster as she realized that it wasn't a bad bulb at all. *Off.*

As the truth crystallized in her brain, the hair on the back of her neck prickled. She glanced up just in time to catch a glimpse of a tanned hand before the lights flicked off and darkness settled in again.

Panic bolted through her, followed by a rush of fear. There was someone in the room with her. Someone standing directly behind her.

The thought registered a split second before she felt the hard strength press against her back and the warm rush of breath against her ear.

"Definitely strawberry."

The deep, familiar voice rang in her head and relief swamped her for the space of two heartbeats before anger set in.

"What are you doing?"

"Smelling you." His nose grazed the sensitive shell of her ear and he inhaled. "Last night, I wasn't so sure because of all the food. The cherries. The chocolate." With each word, a vision pushed into her head. Heat licked across her nerve endings and her nipples pebbled. "But you definitely use a strawberry shampoo."

"No, I mean what are you *doing?* You scared the daylights out of me." She reached for the light switch and flooded the room in blessed brightness. While she wasn't as frightened as she had been a few moments before, there was something highly unnerving about standing in the dark with Brady Weston, listening to his voice, feeling his warmth, knowing he was directly behind her, so close that all she had to do was lean back just so...

*It's over,* she reminded herself.

If only her body didn't keep forgetting that all-important fact.

"And for your information," she said as she turned to face him. "It's not shampoo. It's a conditioner. And I only use it once a week." She wasn't sure why it mattered so much, but the fact that he was so in tune to her that he could smell a conditioner she hadn't used in days was almost as unsettling as his presence.

This wasn't about being in sync. It was purely physical. And it wasn't even that. Not anymore.

"You sound hostile. I even brought you the flowers you forgot last night." He grinned and nodded toward the end of the bar where they stood in a vase. "How can you be mad, darlin'?"

"I'm annoyed."

His gaze dropped and his hand touched her chest before she had a chance to pull back. As if she had any place to go. With the wall at her back and Brady blocking her front, she was trapped.

"Your heart is pounding." His grin widened. "That's good."

"You're making about as much sense as Jeanine Mitchell after three margaritas."

"I want your heart pounding."

"That's why you turned the lights off. To scare me into a pounding heart?"

"Actually, I was trying to piss you off, not scare you."

"Mission accomplished." She flicked the switch back on. "Now get out."

"The point is to get in, darlin'." He flicked the lights off and caught her fingers when she tried to turn them back on.

"When did you turn into such a jerk?"

"At about half past midnight, after watching *Sea of Love*. Have you ever seen that movie, darlin'?"

"I can't say that I have."

"Well, there's this scene where Al Pacino and Ellen Barkin have a disagreement and she tells him to leave. But she doesn't really want him to leave."

S he wasn't going to ask. "What does she really want?"

"This." He whirled her around so fast that she barely had time to draw in a breath before she felt the hard wall of his chest against her back. His hips shifted and she realized he was fully aroused. A thrill of awareness shot through her, immediately followed by a rush of guilt.

*Over.*

Her head knew that, but her body... Her damned body wanted more of his touches, his kisses... everything.

"Your heart is still pounding," he said as his hand came up and settled over her chest, an inch shy of one throbbing nipple.

"That's because I'm mad and getting madder by the minute."

"You know what I think? I think you're excited. And getting more excited by the minute."

"You're wrong." *If only.* While she was angry,

all right, it didn't make her want to resist his touch. It fed the anticipation heating her blood.

"I told you we weren't finished yet," he murmured.

"You're wrong about that, too. We're done. It's—"

*Over* stalled on the tip of her tongue as his teeth sank into the curve of her neck. He nipped her there, not painfully, but with enough strength to remind her that he was in control. The realization sent an alarm through her, but then his hands slid down her arms and he palmed her breasts.

"Spread your legs," he whispered. "I want to touch you."

She resisted at first, determined to keep her body in check, to ignore the delicious heat teasing her senses. But then his fingertips trailed down her belly and lower, and he touched the apex of her thighs. Heat spiraled through her and for a split second, she actually went weak in the knees. Forget holding herself rigid or pulling away or fighting his touch. Resistance fled and it took her total concentration to keep from sinking to the floor.

She sucked in a breath as his touch moved under her skirt and between her legs. He drew lazy circles against the crotch of her undies, right over ground zero. Round and round. Over and over. Until she could hardly breathe, much less stand. Had it not been for his strong arms anchored on either side of her, she would have sunk to the floor.

"Your panties are soaked, darlin'." He trailed a fingertip over the drenched area, back and forth in a maddening rhythm before he paused, protected both of them, then and pushed just a fraction into the moist heat. "Am I making you wet, Eden?"

Sensations whirled inside her and she could barely nod as a burst of heat rushed from his fingertip to every other erogenous zone in her body. Her nipples hardened. The backs of her knees tingled. Her breasts quivered. Her toes curled.

"Tell me, darlin'." His voice, so rich and deep, stirred her almost as much as his touch. A thread of warning went through her, quickly lost in the delicious sensation that burst as he pushed a fraction deeper. "I want you to talk to me. To scream for me. I want to know how much you want me. How good I make you feel. Do I make you feel good, baby?"

*Yes.* The word rushed to the tip of her tongue and her lips parted. The only sound that escaped was a breathless moan.

"I can't hear you."

"Yes." The word trembled from her lips.

"Louder, darlin'. I can't hear you. I need to hear you."

"Yes. You make me feel good."

"Good." He flicked her earlobe with his tongue before tracing the sensitive shell. Goose bumps chased up and down her arms. "Talk to me, Eden. Tell me what I'm doing to you. Tell me what you want me to do. Do you want this?" His finger dipped beneath the elastic band of her panties. His touch rasped against the sensitive tissue of her clitoris and she trembled before his finger slid lower and plunged deep.

A gasp caught in her throat and every muscle in her body went tense at the fierce invasion.

"I…" She searched for the words, but she couldn't seem to think of them. Her entire universe centered on the finger embedded inside her, stroking and moving.

"Tell me." He withdrew and plunged into her again and her body throbbed in response. Her hips shifted and sensation burst through her. She moved again, searching for him, pulling him deeper, wanting him so badly she could barely think. Wanting *it*, she reminded herself. An orgasm. A physical release that had nothing to do with him and the way he held her against his body—so close and fierce, as if he never meant to let her go—and everything to do with lust burning her up from the inside out.

"I can't hear you," he murmured, pushing deeper, wringing a shudder from her body.

"Just do it," she breathed, giving in to her body's needs and the hunger that burned inside her for Brady Weston. "Stop talking and let's get to it."

While he might be every other man in her past, he was also different. More sexy. More handsome. More determined. He wanted her again, and while she didn't want to want him again, she did. The chemistry between them was too fierce to burn up in just one night. But two. Or even three...

The notion sent a burst of excitement through her, but then Brady withdrew his hand to tug at the band of her panties. The lace slid down and cool air swept her bare bottom. The sensation yanked her back to reality, to the fact that she was now half naked.

*Half.* But not all the way, and not with the lights on.

"We need to set some ground rules," she managed in the I'm-a-woman-who-knows-what-she-wants voice she'd perfected over the years.

"I thought you wanted to stop talking."

"I do. Once I'm sure we're on the same page."

A gasp punctuated her statement as his jeans rubbed her sensitive buttocks.

He stroked her bottom before working at the waistband of his jeans. "There are no rules for this, darlin'. Anything goes."

"When it comes to lust. Just so long as you remember that this—" she caught her bottom lip as one fingertip trailed down her buttock and tickled the back of one thigh "—*this* doesn't mean we're seeing each other."

He licked the curve of her ear. "I can't see a damned thing." He reached for the light switch, but she followed, her hand flicking it off a split second after he'd turned it on. "I mean, *seeing* each other. As in dating. We are not dating. This is just sex."

A deep chuckle vibrated the air near her ear. "I'm afraid you're wrong about that, darlin'. This isn't sex, darlin'. This," he said as he bent his knees and plunged deep with one thrust, "now this," he groaned once he was buried deep, deep inside, "*this* is sex."

"And just so you know," he whispered after several delicious moments, the words so soft and low she marveled that she could hear them over her pounding heart. "That light's coming on sooner or later."

Not if she could help it, she vowed as she closed her eyes and gave in to the desire beating at her senses.

Not now.

Not ever, *ever* again.

# 8

"HOLD IT RIGHT THERE." Merle's voice sounded behind Brady just as his foot hit the first step leading up to the garage apartment. He turned into the beam of light shining from Merle's flashlight.

"It's just me," Brady declared. "Don't shoot."

"As if Maria lets me keep any ammo in my shotgun. At least not anytime from February through October. Now duck season is a different story altogether."

"One I'd love to hear, Unc, but it's late."

"You're telling me. It's hours past my bedtime, but I been waiting up for you." He dangled a set of car keys up in front of him. "She's gassed up and ready to go."

"You waited up 'til midnight to tell me that? Couldn't it have waited until morning?"

"You're up earlier than Jesus himself, so no, it can't wait. Besides, that would make it twenty-eight hours instead of twenty-four and that ain't good." He glanced at his watch. "I told you I'd have her fixed before the day was up. Twenty-two hours and thirty-two minutes and she's as ready as Emma Beacher on singles night over at the bingo hall.

"You replace the brake pads?"

"Done."

"And checked the fan belt?"

"You know it."

"And went over the radiator pump?"

"Ancient history."

"How about the spark plugs? Did you change those?"

Merle frowned. "You didn't say anything about spark plugs." He glanced over his shoulder at the gleaming Porsche sitting several feet away in the garage drive. "I can't imagine she needs new spark plugs."

"Are you kidding? Porsches, particularly this model, are notorious for faulty plugs."

"Since when? I ain't never heard of such a thing."

"*Popular Mechanics* just last month. An entire issue dedicated to quality plugs." When Merle looked skeptical, Brady rushed on. "They even did a cover shot of several new Chevy plugs. Real beauts, I'll tell you that."

"Maybe I ought to get a subscription. After all,

it don't hurt to be well-informed. It's just that the danged mailman always comes during *Wheel of Fortune* and by the time I'm done, I'm usually too pumped to sit still. That's when I take out the garbage. Then after that, I'm too tired to do anything but sit still. Forget turning pages or trying to concentrate." He looked thoughtful. "Faulty plugs, you say?"

"You really should check them out."

"That shouldn't take long."

"Then there's the distributor cap."

"I have a feeling it's on its last legs."

"Looked fine to me."

"That's just it. Looks can be deceiving, and the last thing I need is to find myself stranded on the road again. I swear I nearly died of heat stroke the last time. If it hadn't been for Eden, I'd have been as cooked as beef jerky. I'd really appreciate it if you could—"

"Say no more. But this is gonna cost you. You still get a discount, of course, bein' you're family and all, but I'll have to charge you for parts and half the labor costs. This is taking up my time and I've got Mrs. Pinkerton's Buick that come in right in back of yours. She needs a good tune-up and new shocks."

"Take care of Mrs. Pinkerton first. I'm in no hurry for the Porsche."

"No can do. I've got my reputation to think of. Twenty-four-hour turnaround time. 'Course, that refers to each new problem, not the original."

"Your reputation's safe with me." Brady turned and started up the stairs. "See you tomorrow."

"You know," Merle's voice followed him up the stairs, "if I didn't know better, I'd say you like driving old Bessie."

Brady paused on the upstairs landing and stared down at the older man. "Now why would I do something so crazy? We're smack-dab in the middle of a major Texas heat wave. Why would I sweat it out day after day when I could be sitting pretty with a powerhouse air conditioner keeping me cool? I'd have to be plum loco."

Merle nodded. "Certifiable."

"Which I'm not."

No, Brady wasn't crazy. He was desperate. He wanted, *needed,* to reclaim his old life and get back to his roots, to the small-town existence he'd loved with all his heart, and he wasn't about to do that cruising around town in a car that cost more than most people's houses.

He wanted to fit in again. To feel at home the way he had so long ago when he'd had a bright and happy future awaiting him. He'd not only had his family, but friends, as well. He'd been well liked by all. Respected by the men. Sought after by the women.

Every woman, that is, except for Eden Hallsey.

His thoughts shifted to the storeroom, to his latest movie reenactment and the woman who'd come apart in his arms.

And she *had* come. He'd felt it in the tensing of her muscles, heard it in her sharp intake of breath and the low moan that had slipped past her luscious lips despite her best efforts.

For whatever reason, she still seemed determined to hide her pleasure from him. Or to deny it to herself.

For the next few heartbeats, Brady couldn't help but wonder which. More importantly, he wondered why? What was there in Eden's past that kept her holding on so tightly to her self control when it was obvious she wanted to let go?

Had some man broken her heart?

The thought sent a surge of anger through him, a feeling he quickly stifled. He didn't want to feel anger on Eden's behalf, or concern or any of the other dozen emotions that stirred when they were together. Useless feelings, because Brady had no future with Eden. They were too different even if they were compatible in bed. Brady had let his hormones do his thinking for him in the past, but not this time. A little fun was fine, but anything more would be useless.

Not that Eden wanted more. She'd made their relationship, or lack of, very clear. Hell, she wouldn't even have dinner with him.

So be it. He didn't need dinner or dating or any of the other rituals that came into play when a man and woman hooked up. All he needed was Eden, panting in his arms, her voice trembling in his ears. He needed to know that she felt the same intensity that he did. The same desire. The same consuming pleasure.

He felt pretty sure she did but, with his track record, he wasn't positive.

Not yet anyhow.

"WE NEED MORE popcorn."

"Here. Take extra peanuts."

"But they want popcorn."

"We're out of popcorn. I forgot to order it yesterday."

"You forgot? But you never forget anything. I can't remember the last time we ran out of anything. Are you feeling well?"

Well didn't begin to describe Eden's present

state. She was great. Fantastic. More alive than ever before.

And stupid, she thought as her gaze went to the empty space behind the bar where she kept the popcorn. How could she have forgotten a major staple? Especially one loved by all of her female customers.

"I'll give you one word—riot. Peanuts are not going to cut it for this crowd."

"Give everyone a free drink."

"The purpose of the promotion is to make money."

"The purpose of the promotion is to bring in customers. And if we want repeat customers then we need to get their mind off the snacks—"

"Or lack of."

"—and on to the beverages. Those I haven't exhausted."

"I need two beers, an iced tea and a fuzzy navel, and don't forget the cherry in the iced tea. Doris Williams loves cherries."

"Coming right up." Eden ducked down and reached for the jar of maraschinos. The empty jar.

"Don't tell me."

"I'll send James over to the Piggly Wiggly right now. You stall for time."

"Stall? These women are thirsty and angry. Do

you know that Floyd Piedmont hasn't kissed his wife since the Cowboys lost their first practice game over six weeks ago? And John Henry hasn't so much as glanced at Maggie since the Packers signed that new quarterback last season. She's this close to painting herself green just to get him to look at her.''

"Stall," Eden said again.

"I could tell war stories. I once went out with this guy who was more interested in his Chevy than me. Granted, it wasn't exactly a football team, but the principle was the same.''

Fifteen minutes later, Eden slid a fresh jar of maraschino cherries beneath the bar, along with several canisters of Butter Pecan Toffee and breathed a sigh of relief. A temporary sigh.

First thing tomorrow, she was getting on the horn with her suppliers. She'd been distracted during last night's inventory, but it wasn't going to happen again—no matter how good Brady Weston looked wearing a pair of Wranglers and a tight white T-shirt.

Her heart kicked up a beat when she realized he was standing in the bar doorway looking so handsome and sexy and determined. The fierce light in his eyes sent a ripple of heat through her, along with anticipation of what was to come.

"Great idea," he said as he tossed a flyer onto the bar top. "I don't think I've seen this many people here since I got back into town."

"You haven't. This is definitely a record this year." She couldn't help the grin that tugged at her lips. "Jake will have a heart attack when word gets back to him."

"I hear he's hot to buy up this entire block, Merle's place included, for that megastore."

"I don't know about everybody else, but he's not getting this place. The Pink Cadillac is a legacy. *My* legacy. I grew up here." At his raised eyebrows, she added, "I know it's not exactly the ideal atmosphere for a child, but it was the best my parents could do. They had to work and watch me, and so I spent my afternoons after school behind this very bar helping my dad." A smile touched her lips as she remembered all those long afternoons spent eating peanuts and arranging glasses. It hadn't been the ideal childhood, but she'd liked it. The Pink Cadillac had been her home away from home. No way was she going to let Jake Marlboro get his slimy hands on it.

"Jake's offering an awful lot of money from what Merle tells me."

"Not enough. Not nearly enough for what he has in mind."

"I don't know about that." Brady fingered a deep knick in the bar where old Monty McGuire had carved his initials one Saturday night when he'd been too drunk to know what he was doing and her father had been too busy to care. "Seems like you could open up a brand-new place out on the highway, right in the line of traffic. From an economic standpoint, it makes a lot of sense."

"I'm not thinking about economics. This is my home. This is me." She shook her head. "I guess that's hard for you to understand."

"Not too hard. I didn't come back here for the scenery, that's for damn sure."

"Why did you come back?" There is was. The question that had haunted her since she'd seen him standing by the side of the road, looking so hot and sweaty and sexy. "Why did you leave Dallas?"

"There wasn't anything there for me."

"Then the rumors weren't true."

"And what rumors would those be?"

"The ones about you finding fame and fortune."

"The fortune part might have a little truth to it. I had a good job. Good from an economic standpoint."

She grinned. "But you weren't interested in economics."

"I was. In the beginning." He shrugged and wiped a trickle of condensation from the side of his beer mug. "I had to be if I intended to make Sally happy, but it wasn't enough. I busted my ass from sunrise until well past sunset, and in the end it just wasn't good enough."

In his gaze she saw that it was more like he thought *he* wasn't good enough. She saw the doubt and insecurity. The betrayal. Feelings she knew all too well.

"You must have loved her."

"Love never figured in. It was all about doing the right thing. She was pregnant and so I married her and spent the next eleven years paying for my mistake."

"Why did you stay when she lost the baby?"

"Because Westons don't run away from their mistakes. That's what my grandfather always said. They stay and face the music. I didn't do that then, but I am now. I'll face anything to set things right and make it up to him. I really disappointed him."

"We all make mistakes. The key is to learn from them."

"That's the truth. I should have listened to my grandfather. He told me Sally was just after a free ride, but I didn't listen. Never again. Sally wasn't the right sort of woman for me. I just didn't see it at the time.''

The words sent a surge of disappointment through her, crazy as that was. He was only telling the truth. He and Sally had been worlds apart. Brady had lived in a fine ranch house while Sally had lived two houses down from Eden clear on the opposite side of town. Clearly a have-not while Brady epitomized the haves.

''From what I heard,'' Eden found herself saying, ''all you saw was a good time where Sally was concerned.''

''True enough. Not that there's anything wrong with that as long as both parties involved have the same idea.''

''Like us.''

''Exactly. We both know what we want from each other.''

''One week of sex,'' she said, reminded herself, eager to shake the strange sense of camaraderie she felt. So what if they had a few things in common other than lust? Who cared if she understood his reasons for coming home the way he understood her reasons for refusing to sell? Seeing eye to eye on a few things didn't make them compatible, and it certainly didn't change the fact that she was Eden Hallsey, bar owner and bad girl, while Brady was the town's golden boy—wealthy and handsome and heir to the Weston fortune.

"Which brings me to the reason for my visit. We have a date."

"We do not have a date."

"We have a nondate."

"We don't have anything."

"Not here. Not with all these people watching." His gaze darkened. "Unless you want someone to watch. Is that it, Eden?" He leaned across the bar, his fingertips playing over hers as she held a sweaty beer bottle. "Os that one of your fantasies?"

*You're my fantasy."*

*The answer echoed through her head and poised on the tip of her tongue. She couldn't, wouldn't, admit such a thing to him. To any man. Eden Hallsey was the object of men's fantasies. Not the other way around. Even if the man in question happened to be Brady Weston who reduced her to sophomore status with one slow, sexy grin.*

*She fought for her most nonchalant voice. "It could be. Then again, I do like my privacy."*

*"What else do you like?"*

*You.* She shrugged, ignoring the answer that whispered through her head. "I'd like to get back to work. It's not every day the place has this many customers."

"That's not what I meant."

She couldn't help but smile. "I know."

"So Jake's really making things tough, huh?"

"He's trying, but obviously he's not succeeding. Not anymore. I was hoping this idea would pan out, but I wasn't sure if the women would actually come out to congregate while their hubbies watched the game over at the VFW hall."

"Why the VFW?"

"Free pizza and beer during half-time. With the way those guys eat, serving up freebies would defeat the purpose of advertising to bring them in. I'd have to up the offer, which would mean more pizza and beer."

"Unless you offered something else."

"I don't think they'd go for yogurt-covered pretzels."

"They might go for a bigger TV, as in a big screen."

"Those are expensive." She chewed her bottom lip, her mind doing the math and she calculated the added expense. "But it might be a good investment. If it worked."

"You'll never know unless you try. Besides, it might be worth a try just to piss off Jake."

She grinned at the prospect. "He already hates me. This would really get in his craw."

"Hell hath no vengeance like a woman scorned, eh?"

"Amen to that."

"You must have loved him a lot."

"Once. A long, long time ago. But he killed any feelings right away when he betrayed my trust." At his raised eyebrows, she had the insane urge to blurt out the truth to him, that Jake had lied about her. That she hadn't done half the things he'd said. That she wasn't the bad girl everyone had been led to believe.

*Maybe not then, but now...*

Now she was every bit the loose woman the world thought her to be. Her affair with Brady was proof of that.

"What happened between you two?"

"I made a mistake. One I never intend to make again." She retrieved two more bottle of beer and added them to Kasey's tray. "I really have to get back to work. Now's not a good time to hash over all this." Particularly when she was feeling so vulnerable after talking to him, looking into his eyes, wanting so much to trust him.

She killed the last thought. *Never* again.

"Fifteen minutes." He motioned toward the door and the limousine visible just beyond the window. "Me and my ride will be waiting."

"That's yours?"

"For tonight. For you and me."

"But I can't just leave—"

"Kasey can fill in." He indicated the waitress dishing out bowls of peanuts in the far corner before he reached for the small white box he'd sat on the bartop next to him. He pushed the container toward her.

"What's this orchid for?" she asked as she opened the box to find the delicate flower nestled in tissue paper.

"It's a wild orchid, darlin', and it's for tonight."

She pulled the flower from the box and turned it around, searching for a wrist band or a lapel pin. "I don't get it. You want me to wear it tonight?"

His grin was slow and heartstopping, the expression not quite touching his eyes which remained dark and intense and hungry. So very hungry. "No, darlin'. I want you to experience it."

The minute the words left his mouth, the truth hit her.

*Wild Orchid.* He was referring to the movie she'd seen ages ago with Mickey Rourke. Suddenly, her mind conjured a specific scene of a man and a woman in the backseat of a limousine. But she didn't see the man and woman from the movie.

She saw Brady and herself, and heat rippled thought her.

"Fifteen minutes," he said as he paused in the doorway, his deep voice barely carrying above the croon of Kenny Chesney drifting from the jukebox. "I'll be waiting."

# 9

SHE'D DONE IT in a limousine.

Eden stared out the window and watched as the sleek black car eased away from the curb.

Not only had she done it in the back seat of the limo, but the driver had been just a few feet away, his gaze trained on the road ahead.

At least that's what she'd thought at the time. When she'd actually thought. But thinking had been the farthest thing from her mind when Brady Weston had pulled her into the car, and into his arms.

At least her rendezvous hadn't been as blatantly obvious as that in the movie. The stars had not only done it in the backseat of a limousine, but they'd gotten down and dirty with other people sitting in the opposite seat. Watching.

The only other person in the car with them had been the driver, and there had been no indication that he'd had any clue as to what they were doing. Still the possibility that he knew, that he'd heard, had been just as much a turn-on as an actual audience.

And just as embarrassing.

Eden pushed away the strange feeling. Embarrassment was an emotion better reserved for the shy, demure types who didn't have a reputation to uphold.

Eden, on the other hand, was a bonafide bad girl. A worldly woman. One who wouldn't so much as blink an eye at the prospect of hot sex in a limo, much less blush over it...

The thought trailed off as she lifted a hand to her hot cheek. Oh, God, she *was* blushing, despite her determination to stay calm and cool and aloof.

She was far from calm with her heart beating ninety to nothing and cool was a distant memory thanks to the flush making her skin burn and tingle. As for aloof?

She remembered the way her chest had tightened when she'd opened the florist box containing the wild orchid. No man had ever given her flowers before Brady.

And in this case, it was only one flower. One measly little flower that hadn't set him back more than five bucks at the most.

It didn't matter. He might well have shown up with a dozen roses that had cost him an entire paycheck. She remembered the giant ranch house that sat on the outskirts of town. The expensive Expedition his grandaddy drove around town. The enormous amount of money his sister had tipped just a week ago when she'd given Brady his welcome home party. Okay, so Brady could very well buy the entire flower shop with one paycheck.

Instead, this time he'd shown up with a single, inexpensive flower, and she'd loved it. It wasn't the quantity or the money involved. It was the thought he'd put into the action that touched something deep inside her. The fact that he'd taken time out of his busy day to visit the flower shop and pick out something so beautiful and so fitting for the occasion. No man had ever taken the time to discover her true desire. To make it come true.

*Just admit it. You like him. You really like him.*

That's what her heart said, but this wasn't about her heart, despite the fact that she looked forward to seeing his smile even more than she anticipated his touch. This was purely physical and she intended to keep it that way.

It was all about control, and the only reason she was having such soft feelings for him—the fluttering heart and racing pulse and sheer warmth she felt whenever she saw him—was because Brady had taken that control from her. He was the one dictating the how, when and where—something she'd allowed only one man in her past to do. And that man had broken her heart with his betrayal.

Not this time.

They weren't friends, no matter how much it seemed otherwise.

Eden retrieved her purse and slipped out the back door. Climbing into her pickup, she gunned the engine and headed toward the local video store.

It was all a matter of control, and from here on out, Eden was the one calling the shots.

"I CAME AS QUICK as I could. What's wrong—" The words stalled in his throat when Brady caught sight of Eden's reflection in the hall mirror.

"I'll be out in a minute," she called out.

She stood in front of her closet, almost completely nude and oblivious to his presence.

He should look away. That would be the polite thing to do, but there was nothing polite about his relationship with Eden. It was wild and wicked and lusty and so he looked. Not so much because he wanted to, however. He had to. She was far too beautiful and he was far too worked up, his heart still pounding from her recent phone call.

*You have to come over right now. I need you.*

That's all she'd said, and so he'd been left to

wonder what it was she needed. Need in a sexual sense. Or need in a handyman, can-you-unstop-my-toilet sense?

He'd played with the various possibilities on his way over before his mind had conjured a third alternative. Could she be in trouble? Just that thought had sent him tearing down Main Street, his truck tearing up pavement at an alarming rate. The notion of her sick and helpless had filled him with a surge of protectiveness the likes of which Brady Weston had never felt before.

The feeling had morphed into full-blown panic when he'd knocked and knocked, and no one had answered. He'd tried the door, found it unlocked and braced himself for what he would find inside.

*A half-naked woman.*

But not just any half-naked woman. This was Eden Hallsey.

Sultry. Sexy. *Waiting for him?*

His gaze started at the bottom and traveled up, over trim ankles and shapely calves, smooth thighs and rounded hips. His attention snagged on the triangle of fine blonde hair peeking past the white lace of her bikini panties and his mouth went dry. His heart pounded and for a long, breathless moment, Brady thought he might actually have a heart attack.

Crazy.

He drew in a ragged breath and forced his gaze higher, over the soft roundness of her abdomen, the dark shadow of her belly button, to her bare breasts. Soft and round and full, they trembled as she pulled a dress from the closet. Rose-colored nipples pebbled beneath his study and for a few frantic heartbeats, he got the impression that she was more aware of his presence than she wanted him to think.

But then she leaned over, her breasts swaying as she stepped into the dress, and his thoughts scattered.

Everything about her screamed *sin*. The way she moved, her breasts bobbing and her bottom swiveling as she shimmied the material up her thighs, over her hips. The way she looked, with her full, sensuous lips partially open, her hair long and tousled, as if she'd just rolled from beneath the covers.

A man didn't have to be a genius to understand how she'd gotten her reputation. He'd lay money that there weren't too many men who could look at her, clothed or otherwise, and not think about sex. She was the original Eve. Lush and tempting and irresistible. Poor Adam. It was no wonder he'd taken a bite of that damned apple. As hard and as desperate as Brady felt, he would have gobbled down an entire bushel, cores and all.

He was just a man, after all, and Eden Hallsey would tempt even the most devout.

Although the thought of her tempting anyone else sent a surge of anger through him.

Crazy.

He'd deliberately picked her because she was so tempting. The perfect woman to validate his manhood.

*His and no other.*

He shook the notion away. Eden Hallsey was everything his grandaddy had warned him about where women were concerned. A vamp. That's what the old man would have called her. That and a few other choice words. Zachariah Weston's idea of the ideal woman had nothing to do with lust and libido and looks, and everything to do with background and breeding and money.

*We marry our own kind.*

He hadn't. He'd married his complete and total opposite. A mistake he didn't intend to repeat ever again.

When, if he ever made that walk down the aisle, it would be with his family's blessing, with someone they found suitable. Someone with the same values, the same hopes and dreams. Marriage was hard enough without adding conflicting interests which was exactly what he'd had with his first marriage. Sally had valued money above family.

But money didn't solve problems or bring happiness or keep people together. Love did that.

The only thing Brady and Eden had in common was their lust.

His gaze made another long, slow trek up her body and back down again, his heart thundering, his breathing coming in short gasps. She was dressed now, yet he was still rock hard. And growing harder by the minute. Particularly when she reached beneath the dress and pulled down her panties. She stepped free of the lace and his erection jumped.

The clothing should have helped calm his libido. *Out of sight, out of mind,* or so the saying went.

It didn't matter.

It wasn't just seeing what lay beneath the clingy white sundress that turned him on. It was the knowing.

That she'd shed her panties. She wore nothing but the dress. A very short, sleeveless little white number that clung to every curve.

No slip. No bra. No panties. *Nothing.*

The thought replayed in his head as he watched her lift her arms and pull her hair back into a simple ponytail. Her fingers worked at the rubberband and he found himself mesmerized by the soft ripple of muscle in her biceps as she pushed and pulled and—

"There ," she announced, her voice jarring him from his speculation.

Letting her arms fall to her sides, she turned fully toward him and smiled. As their gazes met, he knew in an instant that she'd been fully aware of his watching her.

That she'd liked it.

"Sorry if I kept you waiting."

"Uh, no. I mean, yes. I mean…" What the hell did he mean? "Yes, you kept me waiting."

"I didn't mean to."

"Careful. Your nose is liable to grow."

"Along with another certain particular body part, I see." Her attention dropped to his waist before she met his gaze again. Her smile widened, but it didn't quite touch her eyes. They were dark and smoky and filled with desire and he knew the playfulness was just a show.

"I'd rather you touch, darlin'."

"Not yet." She moved back before he could slide his arm around her and for a split second, he glimpsed the hesitation he'd seen earlier. A self-consciousness that told him she wasn't nearly as in control as she was pretending to be.

"Then why did you call me over here. I could have come by on my way home from work. That's what I was planning."

"Maybe I have different plans."

He quirked an eyebrow at her. "Judging by the way your bottom lip is trembling, the way it always trembles when you're turned on, your plans can't be that different from mine."

"I thought we could go out to dinner first."

"I thought we weren't dating."

"This isn't a date date. It's eating. We just happen to be doing it at the same time. Together."

"So this is what you meant by *needing* me?" he asked as he ushered her out the door and down the stairs to his truck.

"Exactly."

He glanced around and noted that her truck was missing. "You need transportation."

"I loaned Kasey my truck." She climbed into the passenger side of his vehicle. He moved to shut the door, but then she pulled the hem of her dress up and moved to cross her legs.

His heart stalled as he caught sight of the tiny blond hairs between her legs and the swollen pink slit. Then one knee hooked over the other and the vision disappeared.

He drew in a deep breath and lifted his gaze to find her smiling at him.

"So why does Kasey have your truck?" he asked a few seconds later as he climbed behind the wheel and tried to ignore the fact that she was completely naked beneath her dress.

"She's picking up supplies for tomorrow night's football widows' party."

"A big screen is the way to go," he told her.

"If you've got money to burn, which I don't. Then again, maybe my lottery numbers will come in tonight."

"Now that's burning money."

"Haven't you ever gambled on anything before?"

"I prefer a sure thing."

"So do I."

There was just something about the way she said the words that drew his attention. He turned to see her lick her lips before they dropped to his lap.

"You're up to something."

"Actually," she said as she leaned toward him and stroked his thigh an inch shy of the erection already throbbing in his pants. "The plan is to get *you* up, and I think we're right on schedule."

"ARE YOU SURE you want to go here?" Brady's voice drew her attention and Eden turned to see him sitting behind the wheel, staring through the windshield at the building that sat in the distance. "The place looks awful crowded. Chances are we're not going to get a table."

"I made reservations," she said as she climbed out and rounded the front of the truck.

He met her halfway. "I thought it was pure chance that we happened to be hungry at the same time."

"Pure chance resulting from a carefully laid out plan." She grinned and reached for his hand. "Come on."

A few minutes later they were seated in a quaint corner of the steak house. The inside consisted of dark paneled walls covered with all sorts of ranch paraphernalia, from rusted horseshoes to branding irons. Checkered tablecloths covered the tables. Mason jars held flickering red candles. It was Texas chic, if there was such a thing, and Eden's favorite place to eat since she'd first walked in on the night of her high school graduation.

Her parents had splurged and taken her to the expensive restaurant to celebrate. Many of the other parents had had the same idea and the restaurant had been filled with high school kids and their families. She'd sat in the restaurant and talked and laughed like all the other kids she went to school with, and for the first time, she'd felt as if she belonged.

It had been a short-lived feeling. Her reputation had already been established by then and on the way to the car, Jeremy Michaels had slapped her butt as she'd walked by.

But for those few precious hours before then…

She'd had one of the most normal experiences of her life. Growing up, she'd spent most of her free time in the bar. Her parents had worked hellacious hours to afford the mortgage on the place, her mom waiting tables and her father tending bar, and they'd had very little time for traditional family outings.

She'd loved the Longhorn ever since, even though she rarely had a chance to dine there. The prices were high and her income low and so she settled for her memories most of the time.

But not tonight. Tonight was about control and the Longhorn was her place.

Unfortunately, it felt more like Brady's place as customer after customer walked by and greeted him. Then again, she should have expected it. He was the town's golden boy. Zachariah Weston's only grandson. Heir to the Weston fortune.

*Different.*

She forced the notion aside and concentrated on dinner, on leaning over just enough to give him a glimpse of her cleavage. Under the cover of the long table cloth, she slid off her shoes and trailed her bare toes along the inside of his jean-clad thigh.

She'd just worked her way under his napkin when she heard the familiar voice.

"Well if it isn't Eden Hallsey."

"Jake," she growled as she retracted her foot and slid her sandal back on. She put on her most fake, pretentious, I-think-you're-an-asshole-and-you-know-it smile. "You're looking as good as ever."

He flexed. "Owe it all to the Tummy Tightener. They're on sale this week at the Killeen MegaMart. You need it, we got it."

She eyed him. "I guess you're not into pharmaceuticals."

"Sure we are. We've got a full line of vitamins, cold remedies—we cure what ails you."

"No Rogaine?" She shrugged. "I swear your hairline's receded a good three inches since I last saw you."

"I was just in your place last week."

"I know. That much must be some kind of record, don't you think? I bet Guiness is beating down your door.''

"You can insult me all you want. You're not going to make me retract my offer. I still want to buy your place."

"And I'm still saying no. There's plenty of land down by the Interstate. Buy there."

"I'll buy where I want. You've got a prime location."

"And you're doing a prime job of running everyone out of business. But you're not doing it to me."

"Why don't you stop being so stubborn and take what I'm offering you?"

"I don't think you heard the lady. She's not interested."

"Stay out of then Weston. This is between old friends. Ain't that right, Eden? We go way back, don't we?"

"And from the looks of things," Brady said as he patted Jake's middle. "You lied just as much then as you do now."

"What's that supposed to mean?"

"I'm just saying that you probably don't even own a Tummy Toner. In fact, I hear tell you owe those abs to a plastic surgeon over in Austin."

"Who told you that?"

"Hazards of a small town. People talk. You know that better than anyone."

"Well it's not true. It's a lie."

Brady winked at Eden. "You'd know that better than anyone too."

"That was a long time ago. Eden's not still mad about it, are you, sugar?"

"Maybe she's not, but I am." Brady leaned back and folded his arms. "And she's not your sugar."

"YOU'RE MAD," Eden said an hour later as they walked into her apartment. After Jake had stomped away, they'd eaten the rest of their dinner in silence. She'd tried the footsie move once more, but Brady wasn't receptive. "You are mad."

"I am not."

"You didn't have to interfere. I could have handled him myself. I *was* handling him."

He dropped down on the sofa and stared up at her. "And you wee doing a damned good job. Most women would have climbed up on their high horse and put on airs."

"I don't put on airs. I call it like I see it and Jake was, is and always will be, short of some major life-changing miracle, a bonafide jerk."

"I agree."

"Is that why you butted in? Because he's a jerk?"

"Because he was being a jerk to you." Brady shook his head. "I didn't like it. And I didn't like the way Hershell Marks was staring at you from the next table. And the way the waiter kept staring at you. And the way every man in the whole damned place, short of Reverend Skelly, was staring at you." He frowned. "You should put on some clothes."

Her first instinct should have been to tell him to go to hell. Wasn't that just like a man to blame a woman for attracting attention? She'd butted heads with her fair share of jealous men. Men who wanted her.

Men who wanted to own her.

But this was different.

*He was different.* The way he looked—so angry and offended and *protective*—sent a burst of warmth through her.

And so Eden did what she'd been wanting to do since the moment she'd felt his gaze on her while she'd been dressing earlier that evening.

She walked up to him, took his face between her hands, and kissed him.

# *10*

HIS MOUTH FIT hers perfectly. She didn't have to think about kissing him. It happened as effortlessly as breathing. His mouth opened and hers opened, as if they'd shared this very same moment time and time again. A familiarity forged over years rather than a few nights.

The realization startled her, but then his hands covered hers and he deepened the kiss and she forgot everything save the deep probe of his tongue and the warmth of his fingers against hers.

Their tongues tangled and the world seemed to fall away. She forgot all about the rest of her plan—to lure him into the bedroom, tie his wrists to her bedposts with the satin sash from her favorite robe and seduce him until he begged for mercy.

They made it to the sofa. He fell into a sitting position and she followed him. Her dress rode up past her hips, leaving her exposed and naked as she straddled him.

"You drove me crazy all night," he murmured

in between kisses. "I kept thinking of you like this."

"That was the idea." She reached for the snap on his jeans and felt the hard, thick length of him. His breath caught on a hiss as she took her time unzipping, exploring and stroking until he could take no more.

"Stop." The word, so raw and deep and pleading, sent a burst of power through her. He might not be tied up, but he was at her mercy.

As much as she'd been at his the past few days.

"Stop right now."

"If that's what the man wants." She started to unstraddle him, but he caught her hips, jerking her back down and rubbing her along the length of him. His jeans created a delicious friction against the slick heat between her legs.

"*This* is what I want," he said, slipping his fingers between her legs, tracing the moist slit before touching her clit with one callused fingertip. She trembled as sensation, white-hot and consuming, speared her. The cry jumped to the tip of her tongue, but she managed to hold it back. Barely.

The realization that he had such fierce power over her, that he could make her want to break free, to cry out, sent a wave of fear rolling through her, followed by determination. This was her show.

Her chance to slide back into the driver's seat, and she did just that.

She forced a deep breath, leaned over and sucked his bottom lip into her mouth, nipping as she moved her hips, rubbing herself up and down his bulging crotch until he groaned. He donned a condom, then caught her bare bottom in his hands and held her still. "Wait."

"No," she murmured, lifting herself. She clenched her teeth as she guided herself down on him.

Even as he grasped her hips, he didn't try to force her into his rhythm, but let her find her own. She raised and lowered herself, rubbing the tips of her breasts against the soft hair of his chest and returning his deep, devouring kisses. She felt strong and sure as she met his passion.

A woman in control.

Sensation built and the pressure increased as she rode him. The steady rise and fall of her pelvis pulled him deeper and pushed her higher. The pleasure was sharp and intense and sweet. So very, very sweet.

"Damn, you're beautiful."

She barely heard his voice above the thunder of her own heart, but when she did, her eyes opened and she found him staring up at her, his gaze full of blazing heat. He was watching the way he always did, but this time it didn't send her into a panic. She was the one in control. The one setting the pace for their pleasure.

The knowledge fed the fire burning inside her and she moved faster, drawing him in and out in a frantic rhythm that matched the pounding of her heart.

Her climax hit her hard and fast, rolling over her like a giant wave, sucking her under. Her entire body trembled and her legs tightened, holding him deep, milking him as spasm after spasm gripped her.

Somewhere in the far distance she heard her own voice. The sound, high-pitched and frenzied, vibrated from her lips and split open the breath-laden silence.

"Brady!"

Fire flashed in his gaze, as if the sound of her voice excited him even more than being buried deep inside her. But then his eyes closed, his teeth clenched and he arched his neck. He gripped her hips, holding her to him as he plunged deep one last time and gave in to his own orgasm.

Eden collapsed on top of him and buried her face in his neck. He gathered her in his arms and held her.

Their hearts thundered together, one pressed against the other. She touched a soft kiss to his salty skin, loving the taste and the texture of him.

*Loving him.*

The thought jarred her, then filled her with dismay. She didn't love him and he didn't love her. This was purely physical. A temporary tryst. A hot affair.

So what if she'd cried out his name?

It wasn't as if she'd stripped naked and bared all. She was still wearing her sundress. It was just a silly little cry.

The memory of her own voice echoed and a wave of embarrassment washed through her. Okay, so it had been more like a scream. So what? No doubt women screamed for him all the time. It was no big deal.

She'd regained her control tonight and she wasn't going to lose sight of that fact because of a minor slip up.

Chances were he hadn't even noticed.

"*Basic Instinct,*" he finally murmured, confirming her thoughts. He hadn't noticed at all. Instead, he'd been trying to figure out which movie she'd used as inspiration for tonight's seduction.

She wasn't sure why the notion should bother her, but it did. She didn't want him so totally and completely focused on her that he noticed nothing else, especially the breaking of her vow of orgasmic silence.

Yet, at the same time, the fact that he hadn't noticed something so monumental sent a wave of annoyance through her.

"I knew the thing with the dress seemed familiar, but I couldn't figure out why."

"Really?" She tried to pull away but he held her still.

"Wait a second." He stared up at her, a grin tilting the corner of his mouth. "We're not done yet."

"Yes we are. You had an orgasm. I had an orgasm." Boy, had she ever. "We're done."

He grimaced. "I don't know who came up with this one orgasm per encounter rule, but I'm getting damned tired of it. We're changing it."

"Too bad because I happen to like it."

"You know what I think?" Without waiting for a reply, he rolled her over onto her back and pressed her into the sofa. His weight urged her legs even further and he sank a fraction deeper. The grin faded as his gaze fired bright. "I think you like me."

"Liking someone complicates things."

The comment wiped the grin from his face. "And we don't want complications, do we?"

He'd directed the question at her, but she had the distinct feeling he was asking it more of himself. As if he were weighing the merits of complicating their relationship.

*As if.*

His grin was quick and sure when it slid back into place and she was left to wonder if she'd just imagined his sudden change of mood. "You like me, all right."

"I do not like you." She didn't like him. It wasn't about like. It was about lust. *I'll take lust over love any old day.*

That's what she told herself, but the sound of her own voice still echoed in her ears. Loud. Intense. She'd shared orgasms before and none of them had made her scream.

But then none of the men she'd been with had been Brady.

As if he read her thoughts, he grinned again. "Your mouth says no, darlin', but your body says yes." He shifted ever so slightly and she tightened around him, her muscles acting on their own accord. "Yes," he told her.

"No."

He withdrew ever so slightly and slid back inside. Her body accepted him eagerly, grasping him as if it didn't want to let go. "Yes," he said again.

"No." The word was breathless this time, her nerves buzzing from the delicious pressure deep inside her.

"Yes." He plunged again. Harder this time. Deeper.

"No," she managed after a long, heart-pounding moment.

"Yes ," he urged as he pulled back and thrust again. "Yes." And again. "Yes." And again.

"Yes!" she cried out before she could stop herself. She wrapped her arms and legs around him and gave herself up to the delicious feel of Brady Weston.

So much for control.

SHE'D SCREAMED. And cried. And even begged.

The knowledge should have sent a wave of satisfaction through Brady. It would have, only despite her intense reaction, he thought she was still holding back.

He eyed the skimpy sundress that she still wore, the thin white material stretched tight across her full breasts. He could see the faint shadow of her nipples beneath, the dimples of her areola. A shadow. That's all she'd allowed him.

She was still hiding, all right.

He knew it had something to do with Jake and the striptease she'd supposedly performed. Despite her erotic performance for him earlier that evening, he couldn't picture Eden taking it all off for a horny group of teen ballplayers.

She'd been too shy and quiet back then. Too trusting. He couldn't forget how open and wide and honest her light blue eyes had been whenever she'd stared at him during English class. How every expression had always showed on her beautiful face. Her embarrassment. Her longing.

*Before* the rumor.

A rumor he hadn't believed, despite her sudden change. He couldn't quite associate the outrageous antics that had been spread around the locker room to the shy girl who'd looked away every time he'd glanced at her. Even if that shy girl had done an about face and turned into Cadillac High's baddest bad girl.

The rumor had brought about the change rather than any sexual encounter with Jake and the rest of the team. Eden had been hurt and she'd decided to bottle her feelings up and pretend she didn't have any.

He knew what that was like all too well because he was doing it right now with his grandfather.

Pretending he liked hammering soles day after day. Pretending he didn't like Eden near as much as he did.

His thoughts went to her, to the way she'd chewed on her full bottom lip and stared back at him with those guarded blue eyes last night, when she'd been on top of him and he'd been deep, deep inside her.

She liked him, all right. She just didn't trust him.

She didn't trust any man.

So? Their relationship wasn't about trust. It was all about proving something to himself and he'd done just that by making her cry out. Crying, begging, pleading. That's what he'd wanted from her. He shouldn't want more.

But he did.

The realization stayed with him all the way back to his apartment, to the empty bed where he tossed and turned until dawn came and with it, a full day's work.

God help him, but he wanted her completely naked and vulnerable and trusting and—*Ouch.*

Pain bolted through him as Brady slammed the hammer down on his thumb. The sensation jarred him back to reality, to the fact that he'd been hammering the same sole for the past fifteen minutes because of Eden.

"I think she's just about done," Zeke said as he glanced over at Brady.

"Um, yeah." He tossed the boot to the side and reached for another sole.

"Seems like something's bothering you." Zeke hammered a few times. "Or maybe someone's bothering you." His gaze met Brady's. "Mitchell Jenkins saw you and Eden Hallsey over at the Longhorn last night."

"And?"

"And you two looked mighty friendly is all." He hammered a few more times. "She is awful pretty."

"What's that supposed to mean?" Brady wasn't sure why the comment bothered him so.

Hell's bells, who was he kidding? He knew why it bothered him. He was jealous. Damned jealous. Of all the ridiculous, stupid, crazy things to be.

"It don't mean nothing."

"It means something all right. A person doesn't just comment on a man's dinner company unless he means something."

"I just think it's strange, is all."

"Because I was out with a pretty woman?"

"Because you were out with that particular pretty woman. She just don't seem your type, is all."

"And what type is she?" Brady had stopped hammering. He stepped closer to Zeke who'd abandoned his work.

The man held out his hands. "Look, let's just forget it."

"Say it," Brady said. He knew he was overreacting, but he'd reached his limit. After seeing so many men ogle his woman, he'd just about had it with all the attention she drew. And now to have Zeke commenting on her... He'd reached his boiling point.

He was itching for a fight.

"Say it," he said again, backing the other man up a step. Zeke tripped in the process and fell backwards onto a freshly nailed boot. His hand snagged on the edge of a nail and he cut himself.

"Let's just forget about this."

"No," Brady said as he grabbed Zeke by his good hand and helped him to his feet.

Zeke examined his bleeding hand. "I really don't think—" The words stalled as Brady grabbed him by the collar.

"Say it."

"She's just a little worn, is all. I mean, that's what I've heard. Not that I know myself. I was totally faithful to Mabel while we were married. Never even looked at another woman. But I used to hear talk out at Mabel's daddy's ranch when I worked out there.''

Brady tightened his grip and pulled Zeke nose to nose. "Don't believe everything you hear, and don't go adding to the gossip.''

"What's going on here?'' The sound of Zachariah Weston's voice cut into the argument and Brady loosened his hold on Zeke.

Surprise rushed through him as he realized that the old man had spoken to him. He'd finally spoken.

Brady turned toward the old man.

"Zeke? Is something wrong?'' Zachariah directed a concerned stare at the young man.

"I should have known,'' Brady muttered. He leaned over and retrieved the bakery bag he'd picked up earlier that morning. "I've got caramel-covered cinnamon rolls.'' He held up the bag, but the old man wasn't paying any attention. As usual. "Your favorite.''

"You get on over to First Aid and let them take a look at that cut,'' Zachariah said before he turned to walk away.

Brady's frustration peaked and before he could remember his vow to endure the old man's silence, his mouth opened.

"Can't you just say good morning?" he shouted after his grandfather.

The old man stopped dead in his tracks.

"Just once," Brady pleaded, his voice softer, filled with the desperation bubbling inside him. "Can't you just say it?"

For a long moment, he thought the old man would actually turn around. Time seemed to stand still. Brady's breath lodged in his chest as he waited for the old man's reaction. A word. A nod. Something.

Zachariah Weston stepped toward his office.

"Dammit," Brady muttered.

"Sorry about what I said," Zeke said. "I didn't mean nothing. Just trying to warn you."

But there was no need for a warning where Eden Hallsey was concerned. He wasn't in danger because their affair was over. Last night had been Saturday. One full week since their first encounter, since he'd made up his mind to seduce her until she lost her precious control and cried out his name.

She'd done just that, even if she had been wearing a sundress at the time.

"Here." He tossed the cinnamon rolls at Zeke. "Knock yourself out."

"You're not mad?"

He *was* mad, and frustrated and tired of killing himself to please a man who obviously didn't have an ounce of forgiveness in his heart.

For the first time, Brady actually considered the possibility that he might not be able to win back his grandaddy's favor. And with that thought came a sense of failure that stayed with him throughout the day and sent him searching for an escape later that evening.

THE PIGGLY WIGGLY didn't exactly have the sit-down, drown-your-misery atmosphere Brady needed at the moment, but it would have to do. The Pink Cadillac was the only bar in town and that, like the beautiful owner, was now completely off-limits.

As if his thoughts conjured her up, he rounded the corner to find Eden standing in the snack section, her arms overflowing with bags of cheese curls and pretzels.

She wore her usual attire—a pair of jeans and a tank top. The soft white cotton was a stark contrast against her tanned skin. A ponytail tugged her long blond hair away from her face with the exception of a few wayward tendrils that hung loose at the nape of her neck. Her skin glowed with perspiration and he knew she'd been hard at work all day the way he had.

She looked as tired as he felt, and the urge to rush to her side and hold her nearly overwhelmed him.

But getting close to Eden Hallsey was not part of tonight's plan. He'd been there, done that, and now it was over.

He wasn't even going to talk to her. It was better to slip away quietly and carry on with his plans. That's what he told himself, but then she dropped a bag and he didn't even think. He simply reacted.

She was on her knees, gathering up bags when he dropped down next to her and reached for some wayward Doritos. "Thanks," she said. "I guess I should have hunted for a basket, but they were all take—" Her words died as her gaze collided with his. "Uh, hi."

"Hi, yourself."

She lifted a hand to her face and pushed a wayward strand of hair behind her ear. "What are you doing here?"

He held up a bottle of wine.

"You've got to be kidding."

"What? You have something against Blueberry Delight?"

"Actually, it has something against me." She

made a face. "Ninth grade. Tracey Jones's birthday party. I drank four glasses and spent the entire evening hanging over the toilet in her parents' bathroom."

He grinned, remembering the way she'd been. So naive and sheltered and *accepted*. Before the rumors. Before she'd been hurt so badly she'd stopped trusting all men.

Brady barely ignored the strange urge to gather her in his arms and simply hold her right there in the middle of the grocery store in front of the Cheetos display. *Crazy.*

"It wasn't pleasant," she added with a shudder. "One of the worst moments of my life."

"Eighth grade. Fred Tate's Fourth of July barbecue. We raided his parents' liquor cabinet after they'd left to watch fireworks at the park. Only it was eight glasses and his parents' pool hasn't been the same since."

She grimaced as she glanced at the bottle. "I would've thought you'd learned your lesson."

"What can I say? I'm feeling a little nostalgic."

"Why don't you come on over to the bar and I'll pour you a beer? On the house." She grinned. "Sort of a farewell between friends."

"Friends, huh?"

"We are, aren't we?"

He nodded. At that moment, he wanted to be her friend even more than he wanted to kiss her. The notion was crazy, and yet it was true. So true that his chest ached at the prospect.

"Thanks, but I'm really not up to a crowd right now." He wasn't going to say it. Not no, but hell no. "Why don't *you* come with *me?* I thought I'd take a little ride out to Morgan's Creek the way we used to on Saturday nights."

"You *are* feeling nostalgic." She looked as if the idea held more appeal than anything she'd heard in a long, long time. "I'm afraid I can't. The football widow's party is in full swing and we ran out of snacks."

"I thought Kasey borrowed the truck to go after snacks?"

"She did, but then she ran into Laurie over at the Dippity Do. The girl challenged her to a nail polishing race and by the time she'd reached the Top Coat, the wholesaler was closed. I swear," Eden said with a shake of her head. "Those two are going to give me even more gray hair than I already have."

"Gray hair is nice on a woman."

She gave him a what-potato-truck-did-you-fall-off-of look. "Come again."

"Nice." He leaned close enough to finger a strand of her hair. "You'd look nice in any color."

The compliment had the desired effect on her. She blushed and there wasn't a prettier sight.

Silence descended for several long moments as she shifted bags around and tried to adjust her arms. He simply stared at the way her cheeks had flushed such an enticing shade of pink. It was a sight he remembered from English class.

Christ, he *was* feeling nostalgic.

"Where is Kasey now?" he asked, suddenly determined to get her to accompany him to the river. He wanted, no he needed to spend some time with Eden. This Eden. Not the bold, brassy I'll-take-lust-over-love-any-old-day woman he'd come to know intimately, but this soft-spoken, easygoing, blushing woman.

"Waiting tables the last I saw."

"Then she can cover for you. We'll drop the snacks off on the way and you can hand over the keys and let her lock up later."

"I really can't..." He watched the indecision play across her features, along with longing and he felt himself pulled back to English class where he'd glanced behind him so many times and seen the same look. The same open, honest desire.

Feelings she'd had, but had never acted on.

But some of the bold, brassy, headstrong woman she'd become must have figured in now because where she would have shook her head and turned away so long ago, she now smiled. "The party is almost over, and Kasey deserves a little stress for screwing up the supply trip. I guess you've got yourself a date."

THEY WERE NOT on a date.

Eden told herself that as she climbed into the cab of the old pick-up and rode out to Morgan's Lake with Brady. Of course, she'd called it that, but it had been merely a figure of speech. A stupid slip. And this was *not* a date.

As nervous as she felt, the minute Brady stared over at her and smiled, she seemed to relax. She felt his heat seeping across the truck seat to her and the way he stroked the steering wheel hypnotized her. Her reservations faded and the truck ride ended up being much more pleasant than she'd ever imagined.

She felt comfortable. At ease.

And excited. She'd never actually been to the lake with a boy. Another first for her, thanks to Brady Weston. He was showing her all she'd missed out on. All the normal teen girl stuff.

*But you're not a teenager. You're a woman. You know the score.*

She did, but at that moment, she couldn't help but pretend. And with the fantasy came the rush of feelings she would have felt way back then. The excitement. The anticipation. The happiness.

She held the feelings close and relished them as she watched the sun creep toward the horizon.

The ride was short and sweet and soon they pulled up to the shimmering lake and climbed out. Brady popped the tailgate and they both settled down. The radio filtered from Bessie's cab, filling the growing darkness with a slow country song.

Unscrewing the bottle of wine, Brady filled the two Dixie cups he'd pulled from the Piggly Wiggly bag.

He downed his with one long gulp while Eden sniffed and took a tentative sip. She grimaced and he laughed.

"How'd you ever drink four entire glasses of it?"

"It was a dare."

"Then I dare you."

She eyed him and then eyed the wine. "What do I get if I do it?"

"What did you get back then?"

"Kasey's brand new tube of Viva La Pink lipstick."

Brady rummaged in his pocket. "Would you settle for some Chap Stick?"

She eyed his offering. "What flavor?"

"Cherry."

"You're on." She took a deep breath, held her nose and downed the entire contents in one long, sputtering drink.

"Ugh. That was just as awful as I remember." She held out her hand. "Gimmee."

"Not so fast. You owe me three more glasses. It was four glasses, remember?" He filled her cup to the brim. "Drink up."

"If I didn't know better, I'd say you were trying to get me drunk."

"Actually," he said before filling his own cup and downing it in one gulp. "I'm the one trying to get drunk."

*Don't ask,* she told herself. *Just drink your wine and keep quiet.*

The last thing she needed to do was sit next to Brady Weston while he poured out his troubles. She had her own to contend with. But at that moment, with the lake shining in the moonlight and Brady suddenly looking so dark and troubled, she couldn't help herself. She felt his worry even more than her own. His fear. She couldn't help herself.

"What's wrong?"

"Nothing." He shrugged. "Hell, everything." He stared out at the still water. "You don't need to hear this."

"No, but I want to. And you probably need to say it. Haven't you heard that confession's good for the soul."

He shot her a quick grin before turning his attention back to the river. His expression fell. "No matter what I do, it's not good enough. He won't forgive me." Brady took another drink of his wine and shook his head. "Maybe coming home wasn't such a good idea. Christ, who am I kidding? This isn't my home. Things have changed."

The irony of what she was hearing struck her and she couldn't help herself. She laughed.

"What's so funny?"

"I'm sorry. It's just that if anyone belongs here, it's you." She shook her head as the past welled up inside her and where she would have kept her mouth shut with anyone else, she felt a closeness with Brady. An intimacy. Not just in a physical sense, but an emotional one. Because Eden Hallsey knew what it felt like to be an outsider.

She'd spent the past ten years striving to be just

that, and succeeding. The fact had always given her comfort before, until now. Now a sense of longing bubbled inside her and floated to the surface. The regret. The desperation to have it all back again and be the way she'd been before. Soft and approachable and likeable.

"I don't think things have changed so much, as you've changed." At his sharp glance, she went on. "That's it, isn't it? You're not afraid that Cadillac is different. You worried that you are. That you don't fit in, not because people won't accept you, but because you don't really want to fit in. You don't like the same things you did ten years before. You're not the same person you were when you left."

"That's crazy."

"Is it? Who has ad sheets spread out across his apartment when he's supposed to be working in the production department? It's not the same person who used to skip classes so he could hang out over at the factory. You don't like being in the production department."

"That's bullshit. I like it. I love it. I always did."

"*Did,* as in past tense. But this isn't the past. It's the present. You've changed, but that's not such a bad thing, Brady. You're a better person now. Stronger.''

"I feel like a failure." The word were soft and quiet and so full of heartache that Eden couldn't help herself. She covered his hand with her own.

"You left here and made it when all the odds were against you. Sounds like success to me. And you've got courage too. When things didn't work out, you found the strength to come back, to set things right.''

"But they aren't right."

"Not yet. Your granddaddy's stubborn. Give him time.''

Brady didn't want to ask the question that had haunted him ever since he'd rolled back into Cadillac, but he couldn't help himself. "And what if that isn't enough? What if I'm not enough?''

"You're his grandson. His blood. His family.''

"And you *do* belong here," she went on, her voice so full of conviction that Brady actually believed her. "This is your home and Weston Boots is your legacy, whether you like hammering soles all day or figuring out ways to beef up business.''

"It's just that I never used my brain back then. I was too busy having fun. Too eager to please my grandfather.''

"That's something that hasn't changed," she

pointed out. "You're still vying for the man's favor."

"And failing."

"Didn't you learn anything working your way
through college?"

He gave her a slow, easy grin. "Never give up,
even when there's just bologna in the fridge and
no bread in the bread box."

"Exactly. If you want him to forgive you, you
have to keep trying. Most of all, you have to stop
beating yourself up and trying to pretend that
you're something you're not."

As she said the words, he turned his hand palm
up. Strong fingers twined with hers and Brady
drew comfort from the woman sitting next to him.
Comfort and warmth and courage, until the future
didn't look so dismal.

He *had* changed, and while he wasn't so certain
his grandfather would support his new interests, he
wasn't going to give up working for the man's forgiveness.

"And what about you?"

"What about me?"

"Why do you stay in a town that's ripe with
rumor about you?"

"Same reason as you. This is my home."

"Your parents are gone. You've got no family here."

"I've got the Pink Cadillac. It's all I have left of my parents now that they're gone. They worked hard to keep it going, and I intend to do the same, no matter who runs their mouth. I don't care what people say about me."

"You know what I think?" He eyed her. "I think you *do* care. I think you want them to say things—outrageous things—on purpose because you want people to think you're a bad girl. But deep down inside, you're not so bad. You miss being accepted. You're desperate to hang one of those T-ball banners in your bar and line your walls with pictures of the team you sponsor."

He saw a flicker of regret in her eyes, before she averted her gaze and fixed it on the bottle in his hands.

"You're also drunk." She picked up the bottle. "I wouldn't rely too much on what you think right now."

"Is that so? For your information, I've only had two glasses and I'm as sober as ever. Sober enough to walk a straight line with my eyes closed."

She plopped the Chap Stick between them and he knew their conversation was over. "Go for it."

"And sober enough to hop in place on one leg."

Eden pulled a keychain from her pocket and slapped it on the tailgate. "Let's see it."

"And sober enough to kiss you senseless."

The comment hung in the air between them for several long moments and Brady thought for a split second that he'd crossed the line. This wasn't about another rendezvous. It was a walk down memory lane. A heart-to-heart talk between friends.

The thing was, it didn't feel like another tryst. This was different. There was just something about the darkness, the moonlight, the closeness he now felt with Eden that drew them together on a deeper level.

And he could no more resist than he could have jumped up on the tailgate and snagged the moon hanging overhead.

He kissed her. Soft and slow and easy, his tongue gliding along her bottom lip, dipping inside, tasting the blueberry wine she'd just drank. The kiss was slow and thorough and breath stealing, and it stirred him even more than the fierce, hungry kisses they'd shared in the past. Because it wasn't planned or anticipated. It simply happened.

"This isn't ringing a bell," she managed to gasp when he'd finally pulled away. "What movie is this from?"

He grinned. "Brady and Eden Waltz Down Memory Lane."

She managed a smile despite the trembling of her lips. "I don't think I've seen that."

"I have. It starts like this." He kissed her again. This time the kiss was even deeper, more mesmerizing and when it was over, they were both gasping for air.

"And how does it end?" she asked him.

He leaned over and murmured, "You tell me," and then he claimed her mouth again.

# *11*

---

EDEN TOOK a deep breath, gathered her courage and reached for the hem of her tank top. She pulled the covering over her head and let it slip from her fingertips. She wished she could see his expression, but the moonlight glittered behind him, casting his face in shadow.

She could only hear his reaction. His sharp intake of breath as she reached for the clasp on her bra.

Her fingers faltered and she damned herself for the rush of insecurity. But old habits were hard to break and while she was determined to do this, she couldn't help but put off the inevitable.

Nervous fingers went to the snap on her jeans. She slid the fastener free. A long, slow *zzzzziiippp* and her jeans parted in a deep V that revealed the lace of her panties.

She slid the material down her legs and stepped free. She still had on her bra and panties, but as she stared deep into Brady's eyes, she might well have been wearing nothing at all. He made her feel open and vulnerable.

*His eyes.* That was the difference now. Jake Marlboro had been too buy ogling every inch she'd revealed, but Brady stared into her eyes, held her gaze, gave her strength and courage and fed her desire.

She reached behind her and worked at the catch of her bra with trembling fingers. The undergarment came free and the straps sagged on her shoulders. Sliding the lace down her arms, she freed her straining breasts. Then her hands moved to her panties.

He was on her in an instant, his hands catching hers. Warm, strong fingers closed over hers. "You don't have to do this."

"I want to." The words were out before she could even think about them. Not that she needed to. They were true. However frightened, she wanted Brady to be the man to see her completely naked.

She knew that no matter how hard she tried, she would never, ever find another man like Brady Weston. Tonight was their last night together and she wanted it to be special. Memorable.

He'd given her something special tonight. He'd trusted her enough to open up to her, to talk about his feelings. His fears. And Eden wanted to do the same.

"I really want to," she added, sliding her fingers from his to push the panties down over her hips. Lace slid along her flesh and pooled at her ankles. She stepped free and stood before him, open and honest and frightened.

The urge to cover herself was nearly overwhelming, but she fought it back down, determined to stand her ground, to be as honest with him as he'd been with her.

Just this once.

She fixed her attention at a point just beyond his shoulders as his gaze left her face and made a slow trek down her body and back up again.

The air lodged in her chest as she waited for his reaction. Crazy. She shouldn't care what he thought one way or the other. She'd never cared what anyone thought.

But she did. She cared about Brady, his feelings, his thoughts, his hopes, his dreams, his desires.

She cared.

She didn't want to think about why. Instead, she focused on holding her shoulders back, her head up, her arms down by her sides.

"Well?" she finally asked, her nerves pushed to the edge. She needed to know what he was thinking, and he summed it up in one word that sent her heart soaring.

"Beautiful." And then with one swift motion, he pulled her into his arms.

His kiss was fierce and deep and drugging. She wasn't sure when he got rid of his own clothes. She was only aware of his strong touch moving over her, his mouth eating at hers.

His hands slid down her back, cupped her bottom and urged her legs up on either side of him. With quick lift, he set her on the edge of the tailgate. She would have teetered forward, but he was right there in front of her, between her legs, his arms locked around her.

A few tugs on his zipper and his erection sprang forward, the tip nudging her slick opening. He rubbed the head along her slit, stirring her into a frenzy before pushing just a fraction inside.

Her arms snaked around his shoulders as she tried to cling, but he pulled her away and urged her backward until her back met the bed of the truck.

"I like to watch you, darlin'. I like you to watch me."

He pushed into her, a slow glide that stole her breath and refused to give it back until he was buried deep, deep inside her.

She gasped as he withdrew. Then the delicious pressure started all over again with another long, leisurely stroke that took both their breaths away. One thrust led to another and another, until he was pumping into her, pushing them both higher and higher up the mountain until Eden reached her peak.

She screamed out his name and it was all he needed to send him over the edge. He buried himself one last and final time and she felt the hot spurt of his seed deep in her womb.

The sensation, so sharp and sweet, brought tears to her eyes. Or maybe it was the way he pulled her into his arms and held her close as if he never meant to let her go.

Maybe both.

Either way, her tears were bittersweet because, as Eden lay there nestled in his arms, she finally admitted the truth to herself. She really had found her knight in shining armor, and she'd fallen in love with him.

The trouble was, Brady Weston didn't love her back.

MERLE WESTON RANG the doorbell of the sprawling ranch house and stepped back to wait. He wiped his grease-ridden hands on his overalls and mentally calculated the work still left back at the garage. He had four cars waiting and number five was parked back at his house thanks to Brady's Porsche which had been taking up prime space in his garage.

Nothing was wrong with the blasted thing as far as Merle could tell, and he'd been servicing cars since he'd gotten his first job pumping gas at the age of fifteen while his older brother had been following their dad around the boot factory.

Darkness had settled and the porch light pumped out bright light. June bugs flittered and bumped at the bulb, crickets buzzed and Merle waited.

At one time, a long, long time ago, he would have walked right in. He'd been born and raised in this house, right alongside his older brother. But things were different now. Zachariah had inherited the house and the company, while Merle had forfeited his share.

He remembered the day that his daddy had delivered the ultimatum.

*If you go through with this, you can call yourself something else besides Weston.*

Merle couldn't help but smile. He'd gone through with it, all right, and it had been the best decision he'd ever made.

And the hardest.

Even so, he didn't regret his choice. He had something more to show for his life than a wood and brick structure and a factory full of cowboy boots. Merle had the family he'd always dreamed of. The warmth. The acceptance. And neither hinged on his life choices. He could sell his gas station, which his younger boy loved with all his heart, and his son would still love him. Along with the rest of his kids. And his wife. Their family ties involved love not money.

If only the Westons felt the same.

"This is what I get for staying at home while the entire house goes out for a nice dinner—" The words came up short as Zachariah Weston hauled open the front door.

Merle grinned. As much as he hated seeing Zach, he loved it, as well. Because he loved his brother, even though the older man couldn't stand the sight of him. And, of course, Zachariah put on no airs when it came to his feelings.

Merle thought of Brady and what the boy had been putting up with. Thanks to Ellie, who still dropped by for a Coke and a tank of gas every Friday, Merle knew all about Zach's silent treatment and the fact that he had his college-educated grandson hammering soles from dusk 'til dawn.

"What do you want?" Zach grumbled.

"Hello to you, too."

"Hello," Zach grumbled. "Now what the hell do you want?"

Merle indicated the Porsche parked at the curb. "I can't catch Brady, so I thought I'd leave the car out here. I need more room in my garage."

"Business that good?"

"It ain't bad."

"That's not what I hear."

"Well then you ain't listening too good. I'm not rolling in the green, but I'm not starving, either."

"You ought to sell to Jake."

"And you ought to stick to bossing around your employees." Merle dangled the car keys. "Can you give these to Brady and tell him everything checked out fine."

"What do you think I am? Your personal messenger? I don't have time to hunt that boy down."

"Besides, it wouldn't do any good since you're not speaking to him, right?"

"Damn straight."

"Anybody ever tell you you're about as stubborn as a hog-tied mule?"

"Who are you calling stubborn?"

"If the cowboy boot fits..." He glanced down at his older brother's black snakeskin Weston specials. "Those new for the fall?"

"How'd you know that?"

"You might not pay your only brother a visit, but that don't mean the rest of the family agrees."

"Who's been paying you visits? Is it Ellie? I swear that girl—"

"Is about as fed up with your behavior as everyone else. You're a bully."

"I am not."

"Are, too."

"I'm not."

"You always have to have your way."

"No, I don't."

"And you always have to have your say."

"Like hell."

"And you try to make everybody into what you want. Not what they want. Take Ellie for instance. She's the best production boss you've ever had on your payroll."

"She's not in charge of production. She's doing the books."

"Says you, but that's not what she wants."

"She's good at it."

"She's better in the factory, hands-on."

"But she handles the books," he said stubbornly, "and it's no business of yours."

"Says you. Ellie's my blood and I'll damn well

speak up for her if I feel like it. You keep that in mind.''

"What's that supposed to mean?''

"That this ain't just a business call. It's a warning. You treat 'em right. Both of 'em, and that means letting them decide things for themselves. Listen to them. And talk to them.'' Merle tried to hand over the keys, but Zach refused.

"That don't belong here.''

"It sure as hell does, just like the boy living in the room over my station. You're just too damned stubborn to admit it.''

Zach glared. "You don't belong here either.''

"For your information, that's my daddy's picture hanging in the foyer behind you.''

"And wouldn't he be sorry to see how his youngest boy turned out.'' He glanced at Merle's grease-stained overalls. "A grease monkey, of all things.''

"It's honest work, and so long as my wife approves, then it's fine by me.''

Zach shook his head. "When are you going to learn that women are a dime a dozen. They'll ruin a man's life if he gives 'em half a chance.''

"And they'll make it all the sweeter if he gives 'em the other half.''

"Daddy warned you about her. He said she'd drag you down."

"And he was wrong. She keeps me up. She makes me happy. Not that you'd know the meaning of the word. You thrive on misery, Zach. Just like Daddy. He never wanted me to have anyone or anything that might mean more to me than that damned boot company. The thing of it is, that company can't keep you warm at night, or cuddle next to you on the couch, or sit on the porch swing and grow old with you. A good woman can do all of that. But you wouldn't know because you let the one good woman in your sorry life slip away. Hell, you drove her away and you've regretted it ever since."

"I don't know what you're talking about."

"I'm talking about Esther." Esther had been Maria's older sister and the reason for Merle meeting the woman of his dreams in the first place. Esther had followed Zachariah home every Friday with various offerings—a fresh-baked apple pie, a jar of orange marmalade, a bowl of stew. She'd been sweet on Zach since the moment they'd walked into the same freshman math class at Cadillac High, and he'd liked her back. But he'd never acted on that like because he'd been afraid to displease their father. Where Merle had longed for freedom from the family legacy, Zach had striven for acceptance. And in the process, he'd closed the door on his one true love.

After five years of pining away for Zach Weston who had rarely given her the time of day, Esther had moved to California to attend nursing school. She'd met and married and spent the past thirty years having her own family.

"She's widowed, you know."

"I know." At his slip, Zachariah shook his head. "I mean, I think I heard something like that last year."

"She still asks about you every week when she calls Maria."

"She does?"

"You might try giving her a call sometime, if you find the time. I know business keeps you tied up."

"Yeah, well, that's how it is when a man's committed to something."

"I know." He winked at his brother. "It's the same when a man's committed to someone. Only it's a lot warmer at night." And with that, Merle tossed the keys at his brother and walked away.

HE'D FORGOTTEN to use a condom.

The truth haunted Brady the rest of the night

after he dropped Eden off and headed back to Merle's. He'd tried to sleep, to get his mind on something other than her. He'd crawled into bed and closed his eyes, only to crawl right back out because sleeping was impossible. Not with her still on his mind. Under his skin. He could still smell her—the faint hint of apple cider and cinnamon. He could still feel her—the silk of her hair trailing between his fingertips, her hot, flushed skin pressed against his. He could still see her—completely naked and open and vulnerable....

He'd forgotten the friggin' condom!

He, Brady Zachariah Weston, the poster boy for Trojans, had had unprotected sex.

What was wrong with him? He never forgot a condom. *Never.*

But Eden had looked so hot and sexy and scared, and the only thought in his mind had been to pull her into his arms and comfort her. Love her.

*Love?*

Forget losing it. He'd already lost it because no way did he love Eden Hallsey. He couldn't love her. There were too many things about her that annoyed the hell out of him. The way she dressed. The way she lifted her chin and glared at him whenever he crossed her. The odd snorting sound she made when she laughed.

Strangely enough, those were the same things about her that he liked. The sexy way she dressed. The way she threw back her head and glared at him when he crossed her. The odd snorting sound she made when she laughed. All three and a whole lot more.

*He'd forgotten the condom.*

Brady tried to focus his attention on the pile of hot coals in front of him and the branding iron in his hands. He and Zeke had moved from hammering to branding a few days ago thanks to a summer flu that had taken two good workers out for the remainder of the week. Since Brady was the only person with experience in more than one department—albeit eleven-year-old experience—he'd been recruited. He'd taken Zeke along because he felt bad about nearly knocking the guy out the other day, and the more Zeke knew about the other departments, the more valuable he would be to Weston Boots. The more secure his job would be.

Brady grabbed the new boot and touched the tip of the branding iron to the heel.

He needed to think about work, not the fact that he was repeating his past, falling for a woman when he had no business falling for anyone. Least of all Eden Hallsey. She was the classic good time girl. She didn't believe in love and marriage and any of those soft emotions. She was every man's fantasy, and Brady had lived his. Thanks to her, he had confidence in his sexual abilities. Problem solved. Now the future lay right in front of him. A future here in Cadillac, helping his grandfather, living up to the Weston legend. He didn't have time for love and marriage and babies. Hell, he didn't have the strength.

Not after the past eleven years spent killing himself for a woman who'd been his complete opposite. More interested in his name than his feelings. More concerned with the size of his bank account than his dreams.

So what if Eden was a good listener? Sally had been a great listener too. Of course, Sally had only pretended to listen, while Eden had actually taken his predicament into account and offered advice. And Eden had made him feel better. Stronger. As if he really could win back his grandfather's trust. Meanwhile, Sally, with her parting words *I need a real man* had chipped away at his self-esteem.

"Good mornin' all."

The familiar voice intruded on Brady's speculation and drew his attention from his work to the older man strolling through the production department.

Actually strolling, his boots making a steady

slap on the concrete as he moved, a smile on his face.

Wait a second. His grandfather never strolled and— *Good mornin'?*

Brady glanced behind him, expecting to see Zeke over at his station, the object of his grandfather's greeting.

The chair sat empty and Brady remembered that the younger man had excused himself to go to the men's room.

"Uh, um, good morning."

"Nice day today."

"Uh, yeah." He studied the old man. "Are you all right?"

"'Course I am. The weatherman says we're in for sunshine today, but lots of humidity."

"Um, yeah." He tried to think of something to say, to keep the man talking to him. But his brain was still stuck on *good mornin'*.

"I hear there's no humidity in California."

"California?"

"Don't ask," Ellie said as she walked up behind their grandfather.

Brady glanced at his sister and then did a double take, noting her leather apron, a stash of papers protruding from one large pocket, and the work gloves covering her hands. "I'm relieving you."

"What—"

"Don't ask any questions. I'm still trying to absorb the news myself."

"Ellie's in charge of production," his grandfather told him.

"He put you in charge of production?"

Ellie motioned to Zachariah Weston who was busy inspecting a pair of newly branded boots while humming an off-key version of "California Girls" by the Beach Boys. "He came in at eight this morning and handed me this apron and gloves. Said he was having an office temp sent over from Austin to take my place. "I know, I know," Ellie said as she noted his incredulous expression. "We're playing out our very own episode of the *X-Files* and Grandaddy is this giant pod person who looks like a Weston but really isn't. Here." Ellie grabbed Brady's hammer and handed him the computer printout she'd had stuffed in her pocket.

"What's this for?"

"It's the cost specs for the new ad campaign you mentioned to me."

"That was just talk."

"Great talk from what I hear," Zachariah Weston said. "Ellie told me all about it last night and I had her do the numbers before I relieved her of her duties."

"What am I supposed to do with these?"

"Get your ass up to the second floor and start setting everything up," Ellie told him. "You're in charge of advertising."

"And Gramps is okay with this?"

"It was his idea," she said. They both shifted their attention to Zachariah who'd retrieved a pair of sunglasses from his shirt pocket. "Yep, I hear California's just right this time of year and it's been much too long since I had a vacation."

"Who's going on vacation?" Zeke asked as he walked down the hallway, stuffing his shirttails in along the way. He lifted the lid on the Styrofoam box sitting on the countertop and retrieved a venison sausage.

"Me," Zachariah said as he snatched the sausage from the younger man's hands and took a hearty bite. "My favorite," he said around a mouthful. He snatched up the container and started down the hall. "Thanks, son."

His grandfather's voice echoed in Brady's head long after the man had disappeared and Brady had traded his branding iron for a desk on the second floor.

He'd actually done it. He'd won the old man's forgiveness. And his trust.

The realization should have made him happy.

Ecstatic. Unfortunately, it only screwed things up even more. His grandfather was sure to disown him once more if he found out that Brady was following the same path he'd taken as a wet-behind-the-ears teen. He was falling in love with the wrong woman all over again.

But his grandfather *didn't* know it, and he wouldn't. There was one major difference between Sally and Eden. While Sally had longed for marriage, the last thing, the very *last* thing Eden Hallsey wanted was a happily-ever-after.

# 12

SHE LOVED HIM.

The knowledge sank in during the following morning as Eden went about her normal routine.

The trouble was, she didn't feel so normal. She felt sad and empty and *in love.*

"What's wrong with you?" Kasey asked her when she arrived for Sunday inventory.

"Don't ask."

"You're not sick, are you? Because if you want to call this quits and save it for another day, or at least later in the day, I'll totally understand."

Eden managed a smile. "Late night?"

"It started over at Shanghai's out on the highway after I left here. Laurie was there, of course, and she was downing Long Island Iced Teas like they were Hawaiian Punch."

"Let me guess. You had to outdo her."

"It started out that way, but then one thing led to another and we were so drunk, that we both passed out in the ladies' room. We woke up close to 4:00 a.m. when the cleaning lady came inside to straighten up. Then we went out to breakfast together.''

''You mean you had a pancake eating contest for the sacred title of Blueberry Hotcake Queen.''

''No, we just ate together. She had the pancakes, but I had the breakfast tacos.'' Kasey must have noticed the stunned look on Eden's face because she added. ''Funny how close you can get to someone when you hold their head over a toilet bowl while they spill their guts.''

''You did that for her?''

''She did that for me. I've never been able to handle my Long Island Iced Teas.''

''So she won.''

''We called it a tie. So what about this morning? You're too sick to work, right?'' She peered closer. ''Why, I think you're eyes are bloodshot. Are you suffering with a fever?''

*More like a broken heart.*

The thought filled Eden with dismay, but she pushed it aside in favor of hard work. She finished inventory in record time, much to Kasey's delight, and decided to tackle the hardwood floors in the bar.

''We're waxing today?''

''No time like the present.''

"But it's the holy Sabbath. Even the Lord didn't wax on Sunday."

"The lord didn't have one hundred square feet of scratched up wood. You can go on home if you want to."

"You're sure? Because you know how much I love to wax."

"Go home."

"But—" Kasey started. While Kasey hated extra work, she did have a conscience.

"If you say one more word, I'm keeping you here."

*"Adios."* Obviously a major hangover could kick guilt's butt any day of the week.

Eden retrieved her mop and bucket from the back storeroom and headed for the main bar area. Four hours and eight bottles of Mop-N-Glow later, she could barely stand up. She was exhausted, and still every bit as miserable.

She missed him.

His warmth. His touch. His smile. She tried to convince herself that the past week had only been about sex, but it had been more.

In between the erotic movie reenactments, they'd talked with each other. She'd gotten to know the man he was now, as opposed to the boy he'd been way back when. He'd opened up to her and the process, he'd drawn out the shy, naive girl inside of her. A part of herself she'd tried desperately to bury all these years.

She'd succeeded. She'd covered up the pain and insecurity. But in the process, she'd buried her other emotions, as well, determined never to really feel anything for anyone in a romantic sense.

Romance had been a myth. Far from reality.

No man's kiss could make a girl's knees go weak or her palms sweat or her head spin. That had been pure fantasy. Fiction.

Then Brady Weston had walked into her life, her reality and proven her completely and totally wrong.

She'd forgotten her dreams of a happily ever after, but with his seductive charm and his handsome grin, he'd reminded her of a bonafide Texas version of Prince Charming. More so, he'd reminded her of how much she longed to find such a man. Her one true love. Her knight in shining armor who would rescue her from her lonely, guarded existence and give her everything—marriage and babies and forever.

She'd found him. The trouble was, she wasn't *his* one true love. She was bad girl Eden Hallsey and Brady was strictly out for a good time. An affair. A very *temporary* affair that was now over.

As she stood there alone in her bar, the jukebox whining a sad country tune about lost love, Eden regretted the woman she'd become. Because that woman wasn't good enough for Brady Weston. No woman was because he put his family first. He wasn't interested in love and marriage, or any of the things that Eden wanted so desperately, and so there was only one solution to her predicament.

She was keeping her distance from Brady Weston.

HE WAS IN LOVE.

Brady admitted the truth to himself after a night of tossing and turning and getting no sleep at all. He couldn't rest, not with his mind consumed with visions of Eden and his heart aching because he wanted to pick up the phone and call her.

He couldn't. He wouldn't. They'd agreed to a temporary affair. Nothing more and he wasn't about to make a fool of himself.

Despite the tender way she'd touched him down by the river, the sympathy in her gaze, he knew she wasn't a sentimental woman. She liked things up front, out in the open, and she never, ever, intended to fall in love.

*Love makes people stupid.*

That's what she'd said time and time again, and she was right.

Brady had fancied himself in love with Sally and had nearly ruined his life as a result. He knew better than anyone else the amount of brain cells that could be destroyed by falling in love.

Eden would never return his feelings. Not that he wanted her to, mind you. He'd sworn off love himself. He'd just had a major breakthrough with his grandfather. The last thing he needed was to screw things up by walking down the same path as before, which left only one thing to do.

He was keeping his distance from Eden Hallsey.

EDEN'S VOW LASTED a full week, until she ran into Brady at the Piggly Wiggly again.

"How are you doing?" Brady asked as they came face-to-face in the chip aisle.

*Run.* That's what Eden's instincts screamed. What she'd resolved to do. But her feet wouldn't budge. Besides, she couldn't very well be rude. "Fine. And you?"

"Fine, just fine. Busy," he blurted.

"Me, too."

He held up a bag of gourmet roast coffee. "We were out of French Roast when Ellie came downstairs this morning—I drank the last cup yesterday—and so I figured I'd better hightail it over here before she does anything nasty.''

''I take it she's not a morning person.''

''Not before about five cups. After that, she's semidecent. If you want to get her all the way to tolerable, she needs at least six.'' They both laughed and then an awkward silence fell.

''I really have to get back,'' he murmured, but he didn't budge. And neither did she.

''I heard you were living back with your family,'' she finally said, eager to kill the awkward silence. ''Congratulations. Your granddad finally came around.''

''Finally. He's still got a ways to go, but at least we're talking.''

''I'm happy for you.''

''So what about you?'' He eyed the contents of her basket. ''What are you up to?''

''Breakfast. Pancakes and sausage.''

''Man, I haven't had pigs-'n-a-blanket in a long, long time.''

*Don't ask.* She wasn't going to. The last thing she needed was to see Brady Weston sitting across the breakfast table from her.

Then again, it *was* just breakfast. It wasn't as if she were going to invite him back to her place for some wild, hot sex.

That part of their relationship was over. Now they were nothing more than acquaintances. Buddies. Friends. And friends ate together all the time.

Besides, at the moment, the thought of sitting across from him, talking to him, laughing with him was even more appealing than being in his arms.

"Are you hungry?"

His gaze darkened. "More than you can imagine."

"Just so long as we're clear on what's being offered here."

"Pigs-'n-a-blanket?"

"And maybe a little conversation."

"Sounds good to me."

In fact, it sounded like heaven. Brady had missed her so much, and while he wasn't about to try to pick up where they'd left off—loving her or any woman for that matter was not a part of his plan—he did want to see her again.

In a strictly platonic, nonromantic capacity.

*Friends.*


"FOR THE LAST TIME, we're just friends."

"That's not what Darlene Vagabond said when she saw you two over at the Pantheon buying tickets to see that new movie with Brad Pitt and Julia

Roberts. She said you only bought one bag of popcorn."

"So?"

"So friends buy their own popcorn, which amounts to two. You only bought one, which means you're going to share. And one box of chocolate-covered peanuts."

"Those were hers."

"And one box of gummi bears."

"Those were hers, too."

"So you're saying you didn't even have one tiny bite?"

"Maybe one. Hell, maybe a few. Just because we shared popcorn and some candy doesn't mean we're an item."

"Sure, big brother."

"And just because we went to the movie together doesn't mean we're an item."

"Sure."

"And just because Darlene said we looked mighty friendly doesn't mean we were."

"Sure."

"Darlene needs to mind her own business."

Ellie eyed him. "You like her."

"I don't like her." He loved her. Big difference.

"You like who?" his grandfather asked as he

walked into the dining room, a plate of apple pie à la mode in his hands.

"Nobody."

"Eden Hallsey," Ellie piped in. "They went to the movies together."

Brady shot his younger sister a hard glare, before turning to his grandad. "We're just friends."

"Good friends," Ellie added.

"*Just* friends."

She wiggled her eyebrows. "Best friends."

"It's nothing," Brady assured the old man. "Nothing at all."

"SO THIS IS WHERE you work?" Eden stared at the dark paneled office where Brady had brought her once the sun set and the factory closed for the evening. "It's nice."

A large oak desk dominated the center of the room. Shelves lined one wall. A row of cowboy boots, starting with the first model ever made by the Weston Boots Company, lined the shelves. There were all colors of boots, all styles. Only the familiar Weston brand tied them all together.

It was the first boot, the oldest that drew her attention. It had the old-fashioned cowboy heel, the pointy toe. The leather was soft and supple and she rubbed the sides between her hands.

"I like this one the best."

He studied her from his place behind the desk. "Why?"

"It's got character."

"That's exactly it," he said. "That's what we've lost. What I'm going to get back for us. Our character. Nobody knows who Weston Boots really is right now. Are we one of the big boys? Or do we still have our heart right here in Cadillac? We can't be both. That's where we've been missing the boat. We've grown and expanded. We're bigger, but we haven't lost our heart. We're not cold and callus. We're not sitting out in California or up in New York churning out a product. We're crafting boots by hand, the old-fashioned way. The cowboy way." He grinned and indicated the glossy ad design spread across his desk. It depicted a rough looking cowboy. A real cowboy, from his worn Wrangler jeans to his work gloves, to the frayed cowboy hat sitting atop his head. The only thing new about the picture was the boots he wore. Weston Boots. "We're going to play up the nostalgia of our company. Its history. Its heart."

She studied the ad layout and a smile spread across her face. "This is wonderful. You're really good at this."

"I ought to be. I slaved from dusk 'til dawn for

the past ten years doing just this thing.'' He grinned. ''Look at this.'' He pulled out a pair of shiny red cowboy boots. The familiar Weston brand gleamed from the side of the heel, but there was something different about it. ''It's a new concept we came up with for the women's line. A triple WWW to represent the three Weston women responsible. My sisters. These are the first pair of Triple W's to come off the line.''

Eden turned the boots over in her hand, trailed her fingertips over the soft leather. ''They're beautiful.''

''They're yours.''

She shook her head. ''I couldn't accept anything like this. These are too expensive. They are, aren't they?''

''They're hand-tooled so we can charge a higher price, but don't think about that. They're yours. My way of saying thank you for that night down by the river. You said all the things I needed to hear. Otherwise I might be back in Dallas right now.''

''That's what friends are for.'' She eyed the boots again and a smile spread across her face. ''This is the best surprise I've ever had.''

''This isn't the surprise.'' Brady reached behind the desk and pulled out a box wrapped in shiny silver paper and a matching bow. "This is the surprise. Happy birthday."

"My birthday's not for another two months."

"So I'm early." He grinned. "Go on. Open it."

Eden tore into the package with all of the excitement of a ten-year-old. She didn't think about maintaining her control or appearing far-removed the way she did in the real world. When she was with Brady, she lost her inhibitions. He made her feel comfortable, relaxed, loved.

For the first time, she actually entertained the idea that he might be falling in love with her. They had so much fun when they were together. They talked and laughed and...*maybe.*

"I can't believe you did this." Eden stared at the present she'd just opened and a lump formed in her throat.

"Happy birthday."

"It's not my birthday."

"Then happy anniversary. Four weeks ago today you picked me up on the side of the road and gave me a lift to Merle's."

She couldn't help herself. A tear slid free as she pulled the T-ball shirt from the box, the meaning behind the gift as touching as the actual gift itself. "It's got my team's logo." She lifted misty eyes toward him. "Why did you do this?"

"It's our anniversary."

"I know that. I mean, why did you do *this?* Why this shirt?"

"All the other sponsors have shirts. You should have one, too. It's great what you do for the boys, Eden. You try to act like it's no big deal to you, but I know it is. I see it in your eyes when you talk about them, about all the games you've missed and all the sponsor parties you've forfeited because you don't think you're good enough for the rest of the bunch."

"That's not—"

"You *are* good enough. You're a productive member of this community. You belong here. And you deserve a shirt."

"This is the nicest thing anyone's ever done for me." And before Eden could stop and think about what she was doing, she walked around the desk, leaned down and kissed him.

She'd intended to stop with a soft press to his lips, a show of gratitude. A simple thank-you.

But there was nothing simple about the fierce desire that grabbed hold of her and turned her inside out. Before she could draw her next breath, he pulled her across his lap and then they were kissing, mouths open, tongues dancing.

It was a hot, deep, ferocious kiss that left them both breathless and wanting more.

"We should stop," she said, but she didn't stop. She kissed him again, opening her mouth, and he returned her kiss.

"You're right. We should." He slid his tongue along her bottom lip before sucking it deep into his mouth and nibbling. "But I can't. Hell, I don't want to."

"Brady, are you still here? I'm trying to get everything off my desk before I leave next week." The words preceded the loud creak of a door.

Brady and Eden jumped apart and whirled, coming face-to-face with Brady's grandfather.

The old man's gaze darted between the two of them. "What's going on in here?"

"We were just—" Eden started, her mind racing for a plausible excuse. But Brady killed the need with his next word.

"Nothing," he cut in. "Nothing at all. Eden just stopped by to ask me to help coach the little league team that she sponsors." He held up the shirt. "I told her I didn't have the time, but the company would be glad to pay for a new banner for the team if that's all right."

"Fine, fine. Just talk to accounts payable."

"First thing Monday morning." He turned to

Eden. "Say, why don't I walk you down to your car?" Before Eden could reply, Brady grabbed her by the arm with one hand and snatched up the shirt and boots with the other.

"That was close," he said once they were out in the hallway. "He almost saw us."

"Would it have been so terrible if he had?"

He turned a puzzled gaze on her. "What do you mean? You wanted him to see us?"

She shook her head. She didn't know what she wanted. She only knew that it wasn't this. This... *nothing.*

"I need to get going."

"But I thought we could go out to dinner."

She shook her head. "I've got early inventory tomorrow. I need my sleep."

"Are you okay?"

She nodded, but she was far from okay. Her stomach churned and her heart ached and she felt like a complete and utter fool.

*Nothing.*

That's what she was to him, what they'd shared. She'd known there could never be more. She'd told herself as much, but over the last two weeks, she'd actually started to think that maybe, just maybe Brady was starting to have stronger feelings for her.

That maybe, just maybe he was falling *in* love with her. The way he looked at her, smiled at her, touched her, even though they'd shared nothing more than dinner and an occasional movie.

She'd been so certain...

And she'd been so wrong. The way she'd been wrong with Jake. Eden Hallsey had given up her own "lust only" rule and played the fool yet again.

The thing was, it hurt so much more than it had then because she didn't just have a school girl's crush on Brady.

She loved him.

But he didn't love her.

"Goodnight," he murmured as he touched a kiss to her cheek.

But Eden wasn't just saying goodbye for tonight. When she kissed him and murmured the one word, she meant it for good.

"PRETTY GIRL," Zachariah Weston remarked when Brady walked back into his office to see his grandfather perched on the corner of the desk, cost spec sheets in hand.

"Really?" Brady rounded the desk and sank down into his chair. "I hadn't noticed."

Zachariah quirked an eyebrow at his only grandson. "You'd have to be dead not to notice, son."

"Well maybe I noticed." He shook his head. "I'm not interested."

"That's a shame. She seems nice, too. Sponsors little league and everything. Eden Hallsey, isn't it? She comes from good stock. Her parents were both hard-working, down-to-earth people, from what I gathered. You could do a lot worse."

"If I didn't know better, I'd say you were actually encouraging me."

"Maybe I am."

Brady forgot all about the cost sheets and eyed his grandfather who seemed absorbed in his own work. "What did you say?"

"A man should have a little fun in his life. Otherwise, he's liable to end up old and dried up and alone." His grandfather lifted his attention from the computer sheets in his hand and met his grandson's gaze. "Like me." A serious expression covered his face. "Work is important. This place is important, but it's not everything."

"Does this about-face have to do with this vacation you're taking next week?"

"This about-face has to do with the fact that I'm tired of being alone and there's a nice little woman out in California who's expecting me. Me and her go way back.''

"You've got a girlfriend," Brady stated.

"A lady friend. I'm all grown up now, boy. Old. I could have had a girlfriend a long time ago, but I kept thinking I had all the time in the world for a social life. Work was now. It was demanding. Then one day I woke up, and suddenly, I'm ordering off the seniors' menu over at the Dairy Freeze. I just don't want the same for you.''

"But I thought—"

"I know what you thought. It's what I've always preached, but maybe I was wrong. Maybe there's more.'' A smile covered his face as he reached into his pocket for a folded Polaroid picture. ''Merle's latest grandbaby. Born just the day before yesterday at two in the afternoon.'' He laughed. ''A nice, healthy screaming baby boy. Why, you should have seen him in that nursery.''

"You were at the hospital? In the middle of a workday?''

He frowned. ''I can't work all the time. A man's got to relax once in a while.'' His gaze softened. ''If you've ever remembered anything this old man has said, remember that, son. Remember and don't hate me too much for pushing you the other way all those years ago. I didn't know better. I didn't know what it felt like to be old and all alone.''

Brady didn't want to know what it felt like either. He wasn't going to, not if he could help it. He was going to lay his feelings for Eden on the line.

*She'll laugh in your face.*

Maybe, but he kept remembering the tenderness in her touch, the concern in her eyes, the smile she gave him whenever he glanced over the dinner table and saw her looking at him. None of that had anything to do with lust. That was something else. Something more.

Hopefully.

And there was only one way to find out.


''I LOVE YOU.''

The words echoed through Eden's head as she stared at Brady who'd just walked into the bar with a dozen red roses and blurted out the phrase she'd been longing to hear.

The words she'd dreamed of night after night.

From the man she'd dreamed of night after night.

''I'm really busy.''

''Didn't you hear what I said? I love you.''

''I heard you.''

"And?"

"And what?"

"And the general response when someone says that to you, is to reply in kind. *If* you feel the same. Do you feel the same?"

She nodded and blinked frantically at the tears stinging her eyes. "But it doesn't matter because it's not enough."

"What are you talking about?"

"I don't want to be a three-way split, Brady. I want a man who wants me and only me. I want to be the most important thing in his life. You have too many other things that mean more to you." She nodded. "I'm not going to compete." And then Eden walked away from the one man, the only man, she'd ever loved in her entire life.

EDEN'S ATTENTION SHIFTED to the new big-screen TV sitting in the far corner and the five men clustered in front of it. Last week Willie and his buddies would have been down at the lodge watching their big screen, but since she'd taken Brady's advice and invested in an even bigger model, Willie had found his way to her bar, along with his handful of football buddies.

Adding the round of beer to Willie's ever-growing

tab, she walked over and served the drinks, along with two large bowls of snacks.

"Thank you very much, little lady."

"Sure do like what you've done to the place."

"Can't beat a big screen."

"This thing's got digital."

"Glad you like it, boys. Don't forget to tell your friends."

And he did, and they told their friends, and so on until Eden found herself with more than she could handle in a matter of just a few days.

Since she and Merle and a few other brave souls had flat-out refused to sell, Jake Marlboro had finally given up and purchased several acres out near the Interstate. Of course, his surrender had more to do with the historical society, who'd decided to step in and preserve the buildings along Main street. It seemed that things were looking up for the Pink Cadillac. Eden had even started to advertise for a busboy. She'd had three inquiries and her first interview was scheduled in five minutes.

She was alone, hunkered down behind the bar when she heard the doorbell tinkle and her first prospect walked in.

"There's an application right there on the bar. I'll be finished in a minute."

"Take your time." The familiar voice sent a

rush of heat through her and she banged her head on the bar edge as she bolted to her feet to see Brady Weston sitting across from her. He held the Help Wanted sign in one hand.

"You won't be needing this because I aim to get this job."

"You have a job. A job that you love."

He shook his head. "Not anymore. And the job wasn't all that great. Not without the person I love."

As the meaning behind his words sunk in, tears sprang to Eden's eyes. This couldn't be happening to her. She sniffled and wiped at her nose. "I'm sorry, but it doesn't pay much."

"I don't need much. Just you, Eden. Just you."

She looked into his eyes for a long moment, gauging the emotion she saw there. When she recognized the love, the acceptance, in his gaze, she practically crawled across the bar and into his arms. After a fierce, frantic kiss, he pulled away and eyed her.

"Does this mean I get the job?"

She shook her head. "You already have a job."

"You wanted me to give it up."

"I wanted to know that you'd give it up. I don't want you to leave something that makes you so happy. I want you to be happy."

"Then marry me and make me the happiest man in the world."

She nodded and threw herself into his arms for another kiss.

"Is this how it ends?" she asked when the kiss finally ended. "The erotic adventures of Eden and Brady. Is this how the movie ends?"

"No." He stepped over and locked the door, then pulled her around the bar. "This," he said as he tugged her down onto the floor and started unbuttoning her clothes, "is just the beginning. We've got forever to finish the script, but have a feeling it will end happily ever after."

And then he proceeded to make slow, sweet love to her because Brady Weston had found Eden Hallsey's ultimate turn-on.

To love and be loved, and they lived happily ever after.

## HARLEQUIN® *Blaze*™

### presents...

## Four erotic interludes that could occur only during...

**Sexy CITY NIGHTS**

**EXPOSED!** by *Julie Elizabeth Leto*
Blaze #4—August 2001
Looking for love in sizzling San Francisco...

**BODY HEAT** by *Carly Phillips*
Blaze #8—September 2001
Risking it all in decadent New York...

**HEAT WAVES** by *Janelle Denison*
Blaze #12—October 2001
Finding the ultimate fantasy in fiery Chicago...

**L.A. CONFIDENTIAL** by *Julie Kenner*
Blaze #16—November 2001
Living the dream in seductive Los Angeles...

## *SEXY CITY NIGHTS*—
## Where the heat escalates *after* dark!

And don't miss out on reading about naughty New Orleans
in ONE WICKED WEEKEND, a weekly online serial
by Julie Elizabeth Leto, available now at www.eHarlequin.com!

**They're strong, they're sexy
and they're stubbornly single—
for now...**

# THE MIGHTY QUINNS

**Don't miss fan favorite Kate Hoffmann's
newest miniseries, featuring three hunky
Irish-American heroes whose only
weakness is a woman.**

**Temptation #847**
*THE MIGHTY QUINNS: CONOR*
*September 2001*

**Temptation #851**
*THE MIGHTY QUINNS: DYLAN*
*October 2001*

**Temptation #855**
*THE MIGHTY QUINNS:
BRENDAN*
*November 2001*

*And don't miss Kate's
first single-title release,*
**REUNITED,** *which brings
the Quinn saga full circle,
available in May 2002 wherever
Harlequin books are sold.*

HARLEQUIN®
*Temptation.*

Visit us at www.eHarlequin.com          TMQ

# LOOK FOR OUR EXCITING

## RED-HOT READS
## NEXT MONTH!

JUST A LITTLE SEX... by Miranda Lee
SLEEPING WITH THE ENEMY by Jamie Denton
THE WILD SIDE by Isabel Sharpe
HEAT WAVES by Janelle Denison

*Makes any time special* ®

Visit us at www.tryblaze.com                    HBUSCOUPONSEPT

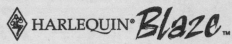

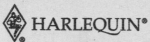

**Brimming with passion and sensuality,
this collection offers two full-length
Harlequin Temptation novels.**

*Full Bloom*

by *New York Times* bestselling author

# JAYNE
## — ANN —
# KRENTZ

Emily Ravenscroft has had enough! It's time she took her life back,
out of the hands of her domineering family and Jacob Stone, the
troubleshooter they've always employed to get her out of hot water.
The new Emily—vibrant and willful—doesn't need Jacob to rescue
her. She needs him to love her, against all odds.

**And**

*Compromising Positions*

**a brand-new story from bestselling author**

# VICKY LEWIS
# THOMPSON

Look for it on sale September 2001.